THE FINAL INGREDIENT

(CREEPTOWN #1)

Scott Charles

To Mom and Dad

1

I'M A PSYCHIC, I KNOW what you'll think: Why would a future celebrity chef (me) keep a jar of slugs by her mixing bowl?

I shivered as I thought about what I was doing. Mom, Dad and Pete were asleep. I had the dark kitchen all to myself. The only light was the pre-heating oven.

Slowly, carefully, I reached for my slugs.

This is for you, Denise, I thought crazily. *This is what you get to snack on tonight, at Sheena McAfee's party.*

PLOP!

The first slug sank into the mixing bowl. The cookie dough swallowed it easily. I moved the stirring stick back and forth until every part of the slug disappeared.

My instructions were very precise.

Foul gurgles rose from the dough. I didn't stop. I kept stirring and dropping in slugs.

My heart pounded as I rolled the dough into sticky brown balls. I set the balls into five-across rows on my cooking tray. Whenever a slug burrowed out of a ball, I jammed it back in.

I glanced at the oily black cookbook page. Everything looked perfect. I hadn't missed a single step of the recipe.

So why was I stalling? Why were my hands shaking? My thoughts rambled.

Isn't this a little too evil, Tammy?

Can you really feed slugs to Denise?

I knew it wasn't too late to stop myself. I could still throw the cookie balls out. I could drop the slugs in the grass, go to sleep, and forget about taking crazy revenge on Denise and the Circle Girls for what they did to me.

The clock ticked. Four o'clock.

Should I stop or move forward?

I closed my eyes, thinking of Denise's smug face. Her wide smile. How her green eyes twinkled when she lied to me. Then I imagined what her smile would look like tonight, when I fed her my cookies.

An evil grin twisted my lips.

A minute later, the hot oven beeped.

I slid the cooking tray in.

2

ONE DAY EARLIER, I had other things on my mind. I wasn't thinking about taking crazy revenge on Denise Daddario. Believe it or not, I was actually trying to help her.

How ironic, right?

My name is Tammy Saris. I'm twelve, and I want to be a celebrity chef when I'm older. I love everything about cooking and baking. When else can you fill a bowl with strange stuff, like sour cream and raw eggs, then squish it all up to make edible food?

Baking a cake is like magic.

I have my celebrity life all planned out. I'm going to tour the world, acting famous and promoting my cookbooks.

Chef Tammy's Top Ten Recipes.
Chef Tammy's Holiday Treats.
Chef Tammy's Book of Mind-blowing Foods.

I also want to go on TV. I think my show would break records.

The only problem is me, Tammy Saris. I'm kind of a house mouse. I hadn't made one friend since my family moved to Hoberville in the summer. I'm not like my brother Pete. I can't suck up friends like a magnet.

So how could I ever sell cookbooks?

Who would buy them? My grandma?

Mom thinks I should focus more on my food, and less on celebrity. She just doesn't understand today's world. So what if my cooking skills aren't the best? It won't neces-sarily matter—not if I launch my career through celebrity.

A celebrity can sell ANYTHING.

As a celebrity, I could sell millions of cookbooks. I could do viral videos with nothing but *pictures* of food in them. My food wouldn't have to taste good, or even be edible. On the Internet, no one knows you used vinegar instead of vanilla, then forgot to add eggs.

Which was kind of my plan.

My web channel is called 'TammyBakes'. As an online chef, I have a simple philosophy. No taste tests. Abso-lutely no scary judges. Just some food that looks normal and cool.

TammyBakes is how I got mixed up with Denise Dad-dario in the first place.

"GIRLS? GIRLS? ARE YOU listening?" Mr. Trevors, our math teacher, poked his long neck into the hallway. "Miss

Daddario? Miss McAfee? Miss Sammler? Classroom! Now!"

"Not so loud." Denise shushed him. "We're filming a pre-Halloween dance."

"Ah." Mr. Trevors pinched his eyeglasses. "Perhaps you would prefer a change of scenery? How about a nice trip to the Principal's office?"

"Aw, you're sweet. But we're fine where we are. Right, girls?"

"*Yep!*"

"*Uh huh!*"

Mr. Trevors was speechless. He had no power to stop them. But really—who did?

Denise and her friends, Sheena McAfee and Maeve Sammler, run a famous web channel called 'Circle Girls'. The Circle Girls post all kinds of videos. Lipsync videos. Prank videos. Elaborate dance videos they film in the halls, or at Sheena McAfee's mansion.

And guess what else?

People watch them. A lot.

Guess how many people watched my **HOW TO BAKE PEANUT BRITTLE** video? Ten. And they were all Pete, so it didn't catch on.

"Three empty seats." Mr. Trevors slumped to his desk. "Seventeen seats minus three is fourteen. Eighty-two percent present is eighteen percent absent. *Eighteen percent.*" He sighed wearily. "I should call the Vice Principal."

I felt sorry for the guy. I really did.

No one else seemed to.

"Nooo! Mr. T, let them finish!"

"I wanna see what they post!"

"Denise is so pretty and funny and cool!"

Mr. Trevors stared at us, like we were a bunch of Halloween trolls.

What can I say? In this world, celebrity is everything.

The Circle Girls were celebrities. They were the crown royals of Hoberville Middle School. So you can imagine how panicked I was when Denise Daddario came up to me after class, suggesting we do a video together.

3

"HEY! YOU HAVE THAT channel, right? TattyCake?"

I looked up and saw Denise. *Denise Daddario.* Her famous green eyes twinkled back at me, seeming to light up my lunch tray.

"T-TammyBakes," I stammered. "It's, um, TammyBakes. Yeah."

"Cool." Denise twirled her perfect black hair. "My friends and I run a web channel, too. Maybe you've heard of it?"

My eyes slid across the cafeteria, to the throne-like seats where the Circle Girls lorded over the school. Sheena McAfee is tall and blond, with thin eyes and huge, clinking bracelets. Maeve looks kind of the same, only sportier. She wears swishy gym shorts instead of tight, stone-washed jeans.

Denise caught me looking and smirked.

"So you *have* heard of us."

"Well—"

"I wasn't totally sure, since you're new. This is good!" Denise smirked again. "So I'll get right to it. My friends and I are planning a new web series. Halloween-themed.

Our biggest one yet. And if you're not too busy, we could really use your help on it, Taffy."

"M-Me?" I blinked at her. "You want *me* to help? On a video?"

"Yes." Denise smiled. "But you can't tell anyone what we're doing, okay?" She dropped her voice to a whisper. "It's about this cute boy I like. I want to film every step of our romance together. Our first date. Holding hands. Then the big, break-up fight at the end. Sheena's dad is a movie producer. We've got all the scenes planned already."

"Wow." I felt my legs start to shake. "So is it, um, a reality show? Or all fake? Who's the cute boy that you like?"

Denise sighed dramatically. "The boy is the problem. You're new, so you probably don't know him. His name is Jake Aberforth, and he cannot be replaced. He *cannot.*"

"Oh. Okay."

"Unfortunately, he's also a huge scaredy cat who keeps ducking our cameras. I think he's intimidated by my huge social media following. Such a pain, right? Don't you hate that?"

"Yeah, totally," I lied.

My heart was thumping like crazy. I looked around and saw the whole cafeteria looking on. Watching me talk to Denise. It was a shocking turn of events for a house mouse who sits alone during lunch.

Play it cool, Tammy, I begged myself. *Don't say anything dumb.*

"So, um, why do you need me?" I blurted out.

I cringed right away. Did I sound desperate or what? Could you tell by my voice that I would do anything to get myself into a Circle Girls video? Literally anything?

Denise's green eyes twinkled. "We need you to get Jake for us. Duh."

"Who? Me?" I almost swallowed my tongue.

"Yes, you, Taffy! You're, like, the only kid in school that Jake trusts."

Denise set her phone on the table. It was cherry-red, with big, silver rhinestones. I stared, wide-eyed, as she swiped the passcode and slid the phone toward my plate.

The screen showed a girl with plain brown hair in a ponytail. She wore loose jeans, a half-panicked expression, and a ratty wool apron she regrets ever buying.

"That's me," I said. "That's my video."

"Check the comments," said Denise.

She thumbed down the page. My eyes popped.

Ur so talented tammy. moar plzzz!
—jake_aberforth13

I couldn't believe it. A comment? Someone left me a comment?

"Jake Aberforth," I whispered. My first fan.

"So you'll help us?" said Denise. "You'll introduce me to Jake?"

"Huh? Introduce you?" My stomach twisted. "But I've never even *met* Jake. You said it yourself. I haven't even *heard* of him. We aren't friends."

"He watches your channel," said Denise. "It's practically the same thing."

"You think?"

"Of course, silly. We're *celebrities*." Denise batted her lashes. "Oh, one more thing. The place where Jake hangs out after school is a little...strange. Sometimes people get scared. They refuse to go in. But you don't mind, right?"

My smile froze. I really hate scary things. Like I said before, I'm a house mouse. I squeak when a pen hits the floor.

"I—um—"

"Excellent! Meet me outside after school, okay? Don't be late."

Denise giggled and snatched her phone back. The entire cafeteria watched her cross the room to join Sheena and Maeve at the Circle Girls' table.

My jaw opened and closed. Denise's last words left me dizzy, and a little bit starstruck.

A Circle Girls video. I was going to help in a Circle Girls video.

I spent the rest of school in a daze, imagining what a boost this could be for my channel.

For me, personally. For my future celebrity.

The craziest part was, I wasn't wrong. When the video aired, it really would be a boost.

If only I knew what the web series was really about...

I DIDN'T TAKE THE bus after school. Instead I wandered the parking lot, dodging buses and cars as they swerved not to hit me.

"Sorry!" I squeaked. "Coming through!"

Several parent cars beeped.

"Where the heck is she walking?"

"Brainless! Just brainless!"

I looked for Denise behind the gymnasium and out toward the soccer field. As the last yellow bus roared away, I crossed the sidewalk and did a lap of the empty school grounds.

I felt sick to my stomach. Where was Denise? Had she lied to me? Did she forget about wanting to meet?

I was about to do another lap of the school, just in case, when suddenly a fingernail scraped down my neck. I let out a scream.

"Aaaaaaahhh!"

"Gotcha, Tammy."

Denise Daddario grinned. I smiled stupidly as her camera light flashed.

"I knew it was you," I lied. "Very funny."

Denise swiped a line on her phone and slipped it into her pocket. Her lips curled in a grin.

"Sure you're still up for this, Taffy? You aren't scared?"

My throat tightened. What was with Denise and asking if people were scared?

"Perfect," said Denise. "Follow me." She started walking away from me.

"Hey, wait!" I said. "What about Sheena and Maeve? Aren't they part of your group? Aren't they coming?"

Denise didn't reply. She sped off, past the soccer field. My feet squished in the grass as I stumbled behind.

"Hey, where are we going?" I said. "Where are you taking me?"

Denise turned left, down a forest trail I'd never seen before. "Hurry," she said.

I followed Denise through a thick clump of trees. Her tiny hips curled through the gaps, like a fairy tale elf. Unlike me. I had to struggle and squirm through the branches that all seemed to grab me.

"Denise, stop. You're moving too fast."

I felt a chill down my neck. I was terrified of being left alone in the woods. The trees looked so prickly. Their shaking leaves made me quiver in fear.

And where was Denise? Miles ahead of me.

At long last, I saw light through the treetops. I put on a burst of speed, hoping to see Denise as I rounded the—

"Aaarrrgggh!" I cried out.

Some monster, some terrible force, was dragging me back to the forest! I almost died of pure shock. Then I wiggled my shoulder blade.

A tree branch. A giant branch snagged my shirt.

"So stupid." I twisted out of the branch with a groan. "Why are you even here, Tammy?" I asked myself. "You could be baking cupcakes right now. On video."

"Yes!" said a deep, scratchy voice. *"You should never have come!"*

My heart jolted. I spun around so fast, I almost snagged on the branch again.

No one. There was no one behind me.

"W-Who's there?" I stammered.

"This is a cursed place," the voice answered. *"It is easy to enter, but impossible to leave! Hahahaha!"*

My blood chilled. I felt like a cornered rabbit as I frantically shook.

"You will never escape. You will die a slow, painful death in these woods!"

I suddenly heard a noise like a car engine.

VrrrrRR! VrrrrrRRRRR!

My face paled. *A chainsaw? Was it really a chainsaw?*

"Help!" I cried. "HELLLLPPPP!"

The chainsaw roared in my ears. My shaking knees locked together. I stumbled backward and tripped to the dirt. Eyes wide. Staring up as a robed figure emerged from the trees.

I saw a glint of red mixed with silvery-white. My heart froze.

The chainsaw blade. It was already dripping with blood.

5

DENISE, I THOUGHT crazily. *You killed Denise...*

My face dripped with sweat. Blood thumped in my ears as I pictured that horrible saw crashing down. Biting into me. Chewing me up like a mouth.

"Noooo," I moaned. "Nooo, please..."

I tried to wriggle away. Desperate, I grabbed for a tree stump. Rotted leaves crunched beneath me. A squirrel gave a sick, one-eyed glare as it skittered away.

No escape.

Time seemed to lengthen and stretch. I shut my eyes, waiting for a sound I could barely imagine. The sickening crunch of sawed bone.

I felt my heart in my chest. Thump, thump, thump. Like a hammer.

Maybe my heart will escape, I thought crazily. *It will smash a hole through my chest and survive.*

I had all sorts of horrible thoughts.

And then, just as my heart was about to explode, or escape, the engine noise stopped. An eerie silence spread through the woods.

Then a voice whispered, "Gotcha, Tammy."

I opened my eyes. Denise waved her cherry-red phone in my face. The rhinestone case gleamed, almost like a chainsaw blade, as a gruff voice crackled out of the speaker.

"You are doomed, Traveler! You will never escape my dark den! Bwahahahahaha!...End of part one. Thanks for listening."

Denise laughed hysterically. She flicked down her hoodie that looked like a robe.

"I collect scary sound clips as a hobby," she explained. "Whenever a person I'm with looks away, I like to sneak off and scare them."

"The chainsaw noise...that was you?"

Denise laughed even harder.

"That—was—horrible!" I cried. "I thought I was going to die!"

Denise's green eyes glinted. "You should feel proud, Taffy. It's actually an honor to be pranked by me. It means I think you're worth scaring."

I shivered all over. Doing a film with Denise Daddario didn't seem so amazing anymore, did it?

I suddenly heard clinks in the distance. Chains? Handcuffs? My mind flooded with horrible images. A second later, something swished through the leaves.

"We'd better get going," said Denise. "This forest is definitely haunted."

I stared at her.

"Lots of places are haunted. It's no problem, so long as you travel in groups. Just remember, you can never cross this forest alone, okay? It's not safe."

"Yeah right," I mumbled. But in private, I wasn't so sure.

"And anyway," Denise added, "a haunted forest is nothing compared to Jake's cabin. Come see what I mean, Tammy. I mean, Taffy."

She slipped through the trees with a laugh.

Lungs heaving, I trudged after her. What else could I do? I pushed through the prickly oak branches that guarded the exit. Then I entered the clearing.

And gasped.

6

"SEE, TAMMY? SEE THE LIGHT?"

Denise beamed as she pointed ahead, at the place. At Jake's hangout. It was a cabin on the edge of the woods. Light pooled beneath the rotted front door.

"Jake is definitely here!" said Denise. "We came just in time!"

My legs shook as she prodded me forward.

"Don't be scared, Taffy."

"I'm not," I insisted.

Cross my heart, it wasn't a lie. On its own, yes, the cabin was scary. Dark windows. Peeling roof shingles. Old, leafless trees that wriggled onto the porch with their barbed-wire branches.

But wait! There's more!

Fake, fuzzy cobwebs tickled my ears as I climbed the porch. Toy spiders dangled on strings, next to toy rubber bats, and fat pumpkins littered the railing.

Halloween stuff. The cabin was full of it!

How could I feel afraid when half the homes on my street used the same decorations?

I stopped in front of the door. A rusty sign clung to the handle. Clarisse something? Clarisse's? I couldn't read the rest of the words. An ugly red scab blocked them off.

A shiver ran through me. For whatever reason, just that sign—and that scab—felt scarier than all the Halloween junk combined.

"Oww!" I yelped as Denise pinched my arm. She motioned to the rotted front door.

"S-Should we knock or something?" I whispered.

"Jake won't answer a knock," said Denise. "You have to walk in and surprise him."

"Isn't that kind of rude, though?" I asked. *Or illegal?*

"This isn't Jake's house, silly. He doesn't own it."

"Then who does? Who did the decorations?"

Denise's lip twitched. "If you're too chicken, Taffy, just say so."

"Sorry." I swallowed. "So, what do I do?"

"I told you. *Find Jake.* He won't run away if he sees you. He'll stay and talk, since he's one of your fans."

"Um, you think?"

"Absolutely." Denise's claw-like grip on me tightened. "Celebrity is power, Tammy. When someone follows your channel, you automatically have power over them. Trust me. Jake won't run away. Not from TaffyCake."

"TammyBakes," I corrected her.

Denise wasn't listening.

And okay, I know what you're thinking. *There's something fishy going on, Tammy. Are you sure Denise's story makes sense?*

The answer is no. I wasn't sure about anything!

Still nervous, I looked back at Denise. Her green eyes were twinkling. And her voice was so warm. So relaxing. It was a rush hearing her talk about fans and celebrities, and to count me as one of the celebrities—somebody with true power, like Denise and her friends.

Have you ever felt a rush like that?

It's like falling under a spell.

And because of that rush, for whatever reason, I didn't want to let Denise down. I wanted to do exactly what she asked me to—even when, deep down, I didn't trust her at all.

Kind of spooky, right?

Denise backed away as I reached for the door. "I have to keep out of sight," she reminded me. "Otherwise Jake might get nervous. Remember?"

Her sudden smirk made me freeze. Was Denise lying to me? Was I about to get pranked, like before?

Relax, Tammy, I told myself. *It's Denise. She's your friend.*

Frowning, I gripped the handle. When nothing blew up or attacked me, I squeezed and pushed forward.

CRRRRRKKKKKKK!

The door opened two or three inches—enough to blast me with dry, dusty air. I cringed and stepped back. Was this really such a—?

"Ohhh!"

I let out a startled gasp. I had suddenly smelled something else. Something sugary-sweet. Something fresh.

It was the smell that finally convinced me. As I stood there, inhaling, my mind filled with visions of cookies and cakes. Homemade pies. They were baking smells. Smells that I loved.

A second later, I pushed my way in.

Squeezing through the door wasn't easy. I'm not a skinny stick person. The force from squeezing sent me staggering into the cabin. I stumbled four or five steps, blind as a bat, before I sensed movement behind me.

A loud swishing? A swoosh?

No. Footsteps.

My skin crawled as I whipped around, spotting Denise through the door crack. She was still in the grass. Far away. And though I tried to relax, I kept watching her closely, suspiciously, until a gust of wind sent me stumbling back. A noise echoed.

THUMP!

The cabin door slammed! I felt a rush of true terror as I realized something.

It wasn't Denise. Denise didn't slam the door on me. *Who did?*

7

THE FIRST THING I TRIED was the door handle.

"Open!" I begged. "Please! Open!"

The door creaked without moving an inch.

"Denise?" I yelled. "Denise? Are you out there?"

My throat itched as I struggled to breathe. Suddenly the cabin air felt so stuffy. So gross. I lurched toward one of the windows. If I could just pry it open…

No. I nearly swallowed a spiderweb.

"Unnnggghh!" I gagged, choked and screamed as something crawled down my face. "Blaaaaahhhh!" I started flailing my arms. Clawing my hair to the root. Spinning crazily.

CLUNK!

My flailing arm hit a shelf. Glass shivered as pumpkins went flying. I dodged them all, hopping frantically, and found myself face to face with a full human skeleton, its skull lit with flickering flames.

I totally freaked. I punched it!

THUMP!

The skeleton shook on its string. Bones clinked as sick laughter burst through its teeth. As I staggered back, one of the swinging bones touched me.

I thought I would die.

"AAAAAAAAAaaaaaahhhhhhh!" I screamed out. "BLAAAAaaaaAAAAAAaaaaaaaAAAAAAaaaaahhh!"

I screamed until I ran out of air. Then I sucked down a breath and kept screaming.

"BLAAAAAaaaaAAAAaaaaaAAAAAaW-WgaH'NAGLLLFHTagGNn!!"

I sank to my knees. My scream trickled into a moan.

Calm, Tammy. Be calm.

Something plopped to the floor.

A spider! I shook my hair again. Out fell…a toy rubber bat!

Artificial.

I looked back at the skeleton. Fishing line connected its spine to the ceiling. The flaming eyes were electric, and the laugh was a tinny recording.

I shook my head in embarrassment. Junk. It was all Halloween junk! Even the light on the porch was a prop. Someone had left a flashlight switched on by the door.

But who? Who would do that?

My brow furrowed. I would've definitely figured it out, even without the sounds rising up from the porch. Sounds I recognized.

The clink of Sheena McAfee's bracelets.

The swish of Maeve Sammler's gym shorts.

The laughter—the shrill, shaking laughter—of Denise Daddario as she congratulated her two drones on the perfect prank they'd just pulled.

"I filmed it! I filmed it all!" Sheena crowed.

23

"Should we let her out now?" Maeve whispered.

"Not yet. Let's try scraping the wood first."

Denise. I gnashed my teeth as an 'eerie' scraping noise shot up the walls. My pounding heart filled with hate. It was all a setup. All fake!

Of course it was fake, Tammy. Did you really think Denise Daddario was your friend? That she wouldn't try tricking you? Are you that dumb?

I looked around again. I couldn't believe I'd freaked out over a bunch of Halloween junk that wasn't even scary. From their loud voices, I knew the Circle Girls had planted the decorations themselves. That explained why they felt so out of place in the cabin.

Denise probably thinks she's so smart, I thought angrily. *Does she think her stupid toy spiders were scary? I only screamed because I couldn't see them! And what did they say about film? Are they FILMING me?*

"Great," I muttered. "Just great."

My blood boiled. I imagined the Circle Girls hiding out on the porch. Waiting for me to panic. To pound my fists on the wall. To beg and plead to escape out the door that they'd slammed on me.

I won't let them win, I decided. *I'll just sit here. Sit forever. And later, if Denise tries to peek in and check on me...*

My lip curled in an evil grin. I pictured Sheena and Maeve dropping their phones as I leapt out and scared them. Denise wouldn't be laughing then. She'd be screaming!

I rubbed my hands together. *The perfect revenge.*

Feeling calmer already, I found a spot in the corner and sat. I kept as quiet as possible. No footsteps. No heavy breathing. I didn't want Denise or her drones to hear anything.

That's when the sugary smell wafted in.

My nose crinkled. I looked again at the cabin, squinting at the domed platters and dusty glass shelves. Were there items still in them?

I leaned closer.

Yes. Name and price tags. Some stale-looking crumbs.

My heart fluttered. A bakery? Was I trapped inside of a bakery?

I reached toward a shelf. My hand bumped something solid. A narrow black book.

The cabin walls thumped all around me. The Circle Girls were still laughing their heads off. I couldn't wait to turn the tables and scare them.

But first, I dragged the book off the shelf and examined it. I still don't know why. Curiosity? Oil dripped down the spine as I stared at it.

THE BOOKE OF LOSTE FOODES

I held my breath as I opened it. There were very few pages. Each page was ink-black, with pale writing I couldn't decipher. The text seemed to slither and change as my brain fought to read it.

The only legible words were up top.

CHILLER COOKIES
THE FIRST GRAND DESSERT

"A cookbook?" I said. "A *Halloween* cookbook?"

"Close enough." A voice echoed behind me. I whipped around.

"W-Who's there?"

When no one spoke, I put my hand on my heart, calming down.

A recording. Another stupid recording.

"I'm going to kill Denise when I see her," I grumbled.

"Sounds like a plan. Want some help?"

A light flickered. Something moved in the shadows.

A person. A boy.

Climbing out of the rotted wood wall.

"Hey stranger," said the voice. "Nice to meet you. I'm Jake."

.8

MY JAW DROPPED. The last person I expected to see was Jake Aberforth.

So Jake was real? He was here?

Denise Daddario hadn't been lying...

It wasn't love at first sight. I wasn't obsessed with Jake's crisp, light-blue eyes. His endlessly wavy brown hair. Or the sugary scent of his—

"Hem hem." Jake cleared his throat softly. "For someone breaking into my cabin," he said, "you seem pretty high-strung."

My heart jolted. "*YOUR* cabin? But Denise told me—she said it wasn't—that nobody—"

"Just messing with you, stranger." Jake laughed.

"Tammy," I said shakily. "Call me Tammy."

"I'm Jake," said Jake, stepping forward. As he did, I noticed the wall behind him was hiding a staircase. How crazy was I, thinking he'd climbed off a wall?

My skin shivered anyway. "Hang on," I said suspiciously. "Did Denise Daddario bring you here? Are you helping her? Because I won't fall for a prank again. Don't even try."

Jake shrugged. "Sometimes people ask me to do things, but that doesn't mean that I help them. If it's not about cooking or baking, I just zone them out." He touched his brown hair and grinned. "You're a chef, aren't you, Tammy?"

I blinked. "How did you—?"

"I read minds. That, and I saw the cookbook you're reading."

We both laughed.

"Sometimes I pretend I'm a psychic," I admitted.

"Cute. That's adorable."

My cheeks flushed. "jake_aberforth13," I said suddenly. "Is that you? On the Internet, I mean. Do you follow my TammyBakes channel?"

Jake didn't deny it. "I follow everything to do with baking, Tammy. You could say I'm obsessed."

Me too, I thought.

"Unfortunately, I don't often bake anymore," Jake went on. "Not since the accident."

My face paled. "The accident?"

"That's right. I was experimenting with a new recipe. At the critical moment, I lost my nerve and screwed up." Jake sighed. "Mother will never forgive me. I swore I would finish her cookbook. But I can't anymore. I just can't."

"Oh gosh, I'm so sorry—"

"But you can." Jake's reply was so swift, my skin prickled. He nodded to the book in my lap.

"Huh?" I said. "The Halloween cookbook?"

28

"*The Booke of Loste Foodes,*" Jake corrected. "It belonged to Mother, once. Then she passed it to me."

I felt really confused.

"Chiller Cookies," I said. "You're saying that's a serious recipe?"

"Deadly serious. Yes."

My eyes scrunched. This was a joke, right? If anyone else tried to tell me the Halloween cookbook was real, I would've called them a liar.

But Jake seemed so honest. So sweet. I didn't think he would lie to me. Or maybe I just *wanted* Jake to be telling the truth. Entrusting me with his secrets. Requesting my help.

Me. Tammy Saris.

Assistant and friend to Jake Aberforth. Boy.

"Help me, Tammy," Jake whispered. "Promise you'll take *The Booke of Loste Foodes* and complete all the recipes."

"Huh? Complete them? With you?"

"Not at first. This is your project, Tammy." Jake grinned at me. "You'll enjoy it, though. Mother's desserts are quite good. If you bake them correctly, you'll get all kinds of benefits."

"Benefits?" I said uncertainly.

Jake dropped his voice to a whisper. *"Beyond your wildest dreams."*

His light-blue eyes glittered. He leaned close, releasing a fresh wave of sugary sweetness. "You want to be famous, don't you, Tammy? A celebrity chef. One of the greats."

My throat spasmed. How did he——?

"I read minds," Jake repeated.

This time, neither one of us laughed. I felt cold shivers as Jake made a lunge for my hand.

No. For *The Booke.*

Something shuddered inside of its pages.

"Are you ready, Tammy?" Jake whispered, retracting his hand. "Will you swear to complete Mother's cookbook?"

A shiver ran through me. Jake's light-blue eyes seemed a little too bright all the sudden. A little too focused. Then again, he still had his smile. His sugary sweetness. His cheekbones.

Did I mention his cheekbones?

Heart thudding, I laid my palm on *The Booke of Loste Foodes.* I tried to pass everything off as a joke.

"I solemnly swear I am up to no good."

Jake's smile withered and died. *"Don't joke around. Make the vow!"*

His ringing tone really shocked me. He seemed to notice it, too.

"S-Sorry," he said quickly. "I just—it's a sensitive topic. My mother. *The Booke.* You understand, don't you, Tammy?"

I scrunched my eyes again. *Did I?*

I understood that Jake Aberforth was the first boy my age I'd ever talked to for more than five minutes. He was also a chef. He liked cooking and baking—

And me.

God help me.

I closed my eyes as Jake walked me through the vow process. I spoke all sorts of words. It was easier the second time around. Jake was calmer now. He even cracked jokes.

I barely noticed when the cabin air trembled. A fizzing noise rose from *The Booke*, making me gasp and open my eyes.

Wait. Where was Jake?

"Jake?" I called out. "Jake?"

I craned around in the gloom. Feeling panicked.

"Jake? Hey, Jake? Where'd you—?"

BOOOOOOOMMMMM!

A thunderous noise blasted over the cabin. Dust spilled from the rafters as fresh laughter rose from the skeleton. I spun around, toward the source of the blast: a huge, glowing gap in the wood—

Filled by three vicious monsters. Three beasts.

"Give it to meeee!" they cried.

"Give us the booooookkkk!"

"It issss ourrssss!"

·9

ON ANOTHER DAY, I would've spotted them instantly: Sheena, Maeve and Denise, all in demon masks; the sunny gap where the cabin door opened; also, their cell phones. Their cell phones!

But in that moment, as the three demons whooped and rushed in, I was too distracted. Too shaken up. Too confused by Jake's absence.

"KABBLAAAaaaAAAAaaaaAAAAaaahhHHHHH!"

I screamed until my lungs were ripped raw. The Circle Girls tore off their masks. They looked even more vicious without them.

"It's perfect! The perfect ending!"

"The book part was genius! She really was holding a book!"

"I know! I just blurted it out! But then Maeve had to copy me."

"Whatever, Sheena!"

The Circle Girls dissolved into giggles. They barely looked at me. A minute passed before Denise fluffed her perfect black hair, looking up.

"Gotcha, Tammy."

Beside her, Sheena and Maeve's phones flashed with crisp, high-def pictures. I winced as I heard myself scream, more than once.

"Great, isn't it?" Sheena smirked.

"The best stuff is on the hidden cameras inside," said Maeve. "She was ranting and raving in there. I can't wait to hear what she said."

I cleared my throat loudly. "Hidden cameras?"

The Circle Girls grinned at me.

So that's why they left me in the cabin so long. Hidden cameras! Even if they couldn't see me, they knew I was being recorded.

I thought back to those cobwebs. The toy spiders. My little dance with that horrible skeleton.

All on video. My blood boiled.

"Uh oh, I think Taffy just figured it out!" said Denise, as Sheena and Maeve giggled.

That's when I knew, without doubt, that they'd been filming me from the very beginning. The clinking, swishing sounds in the woods only proved it. Denise was probably late to our meeting because she was giving orders to Sheena and Maeve.

Having them follow us into the forest.

Or were they already there, in the trees?

"Did you enjoy the cabin?" Denise asked me. "Was it nice inside? Did you talk to Jake Aberforth?"

I put on my bravest expression.

"The cabin was fine," I said. "Actually, the decorations helped me relax. There's nothing scary about pumpkins and bats. I only screamed at the end because you interrupted Jake and me talking."

The Circle Girls swiveled their heads.

"Jake Aberforth?"

"You really saw Jake?"

I nodded. "He ran off when you barged in the door."

Denise's eyes glimmered. She suddenly let out a cackle.

"I cannot *wait* to see what the hidden cameras picked up!"

"Maybe Jake will be on them," said Sheena.

"If he is, we'll be even more famous," Maeve giggled.

The Booke of Loste Foodes suddenly slipped from my fingers. I gasped as Denise spun away with it, grinning.

"Oooh, it's a book! Taffy's freaky black book!"

"Give it back!"

"Oh? A cookbook!" Denise started thumbing the pages. "Let's see what horrible stuff Taffy bakes!"

Frantic, I lunged for *The Booke*. Unsuccessfully.

"Hmmm. Wheat germ. Baking powder. Vanilla extract. *Oh my God.* SLUGS! WILD SLUGS! I'm not even kidding, you guys. It really says slugs!"

Sheena and Maeve scurried over. Their eyes stretched as they swept down the page. They couldn't stop laughing.

"Is this a family recipe, Tammy?"

"No wonder your channel has, like, negative viewers!"

"Give it back!" I demanded. "It isn't even mine. It belongs to Jake Aberforth!"

The Circle Girls laughed even harder. Sheena and Maeve pulled their cell phones out. Recording me.

Ugh.

I grabbed *The Booke of Loste Foodes* from Denise and thumbed through it. I knew I wouldn't be able to read the weird writing. So I was pretty surprised when I realized I could. Maybe the sunlight was helping me?

My eyes swept through the Chiller Cookies recipe. I was looking for weird stuff. Things like that. However, the instructions looked totally normal.

Stupid Denise, I thought. *Always making stuff up.*

I kept skimming the page, just in case. That's when my eyes fell on two scratchy lines in a box at the end. My smile froze.

FINAL INGREDIENT ALERT!
SLUGS (WILD, 32CT.)

"What the—?"

A sick feeling twisted my stomach. *Slugs? Wild slugs?* I read the page again. This time, I noticed other odd features. Stuff I'd spotted before, but dismissed, like the solid black pages. How oily they felt. But also how brittle. How tough.

I read the title again.

Chiller Cookies.

The last puzzle piece clicked into place.

Fake. It was fake! *The Booke of Loste Foodes* was just another dumb prop, like the pumpkins and bats.

Halloween junk!

My thoughts flared. Did that mean Jake Aberforth was part of the joke? Was his story a lie? Was he...pranking me?

CRRRRRNNNNNCHHH!

A sudden noise jerked me out of my thoughts. Looking up, I saw what, at first, looked like a pearly-white space shuttle. Gravel stirred as it drifted to Earth, from the Southern Crab Nebula—okay, from boring old Highway 13—then onto a slip road that curved through the trees, toward the lawn where we stood.

A limo. A pearly-white limousine.

Sheena stalked toward the driver's side window.

"You're not stretch," she complained. "Why aren't you stretch?"

Maeve and Denise trotted over.

"Is this our ride?"

"Awesome birthday gift, Sheena."

"It's not the model I wanted," Sheena moaned. "Or a Hummer."

Maeve giggled. "What should we do about You-Know-Who?"

"Leave her," said Sheena. "She's filthy. She walked in that cabin!"

"Will we get in trouble, though? Ditching her?"

"Do I actually care, though?"

Sheena's driver held the door as the Circle Girls clambered inside.

"Coming, Miss?" the driver asked me. "It's getting late."

Sheena scowled. "I *guess* we could drop her off last," she said lamely.

"Can she fit in the trunk?" laughed Denise.

My blood boiled all over again. "Forget it," I spat. "I'd rather walk than ride anyway." I spun on my heel, letting the fake cookbook drop to the dirt. "Keep it. Better yet, keep all your dumb decorations. Next time, you can prank someone else. Leave me out of it!"

Sheena's stretch limousine seemed to giggle—and crunch—as it rolled toward the street, out of sight.

I clenched my jaw angrily. *Forget viral videos,* I thought. *I'm done with them. And I'm done with stupid Denise and the Circle Girls.*

But it wasn't the truth.

Not even close.

10

DID I TAKE THE forest trail back, all alone?

No. Denise might be a twinkly-eyed liar, but I wasn't sure if she lied about the woods being haunted. That trail was too creepy. I never wanted to go back there.

Instead, I trudged through a ditch along Highway 13. One of my neighbors, Mrs. Johns, picked me up in her Honda.

Ten minutes later, I slammed through the door of my house. The walls shook and the ceiling lights flickered.

"Run, run for your lives!" Mom cried out. "It's Hurricane Tammy!"

Dad held his laptop case over Mom's head. Stale Cheetos rained on their heads. Mom pretended to gasp, like someone pelted by hail.

My parents have a strange sense of humor. They're both computer programmers who work from home. I'm not sure if the two are connected. But probably.

"Food!" shouted Pete. My little brother threw himself onto the floor like a terrier, biting and clawing the Cheetos. He even barked like a dog.

"Chill, Pete," I said. "I'll bake you brownies if you stop barking, okay?"

Pete clutched his throat and made choking sounds.

"Dead. I'm dead. Tammy poisoned me."

"Oh shut up. You love brownies."

"Real brownies. Not disgusting Tammy brownies."

"You still ate them," I grumbled.

Dad stood up and pressed a baseball glove into Pete's ribs.

"What do you say, Pete? Are you human enough for a catch?"

"RUFF!"

Dad and Pete disappeared into the garage. I tried to slip upstairs, but Mom pulled me into a hug.

"Tammy, hey. Don't blow away. How was school?" Mom stared at me through her winged eyeglasses. "Hmm. Let me guess. Strong winds and flash flooding? I see the hurricane shut down the grocery store."

My face fell. "Oh man, I forgot to buy groceries!"

"Lucky for you, I checked the forecast this morning."

Mom gripped my shoulders and spun me into the dining room. Fresh groceries lay on the table. Mostly baking supplies, which I desperately needed.

I sighed with relief. Mom is my biggest TammyBakes fan (so far).

"You'll have to unpack them yourself, though." Mom salsa-danced through the door Pete left open. "The Limber Ladies should be passing the house any minute. Wooo!"

I rolled my eyes. "The Limber Ladies? Does your walking group know you call them that?"

"Nope! In front of them, it's The Old Bags." Mom jiggled her arm in a wave. "Don't fret about dinner, sweetie. Your dad has a plan. But if you want to bake your famous sour brownies, go ahead. Pete will eat anything."

Mom smiled and skipped out the door.

"They're not sour on purpose," I mumbled.

I grabbed the groceries and marched to the kitchen. It was eerily quiet without Mom, Dad or Pete. The only sound was the POP! POP! POP! of Dad's catcher's mitt. Then a loud SPLOOOSH! as a ball hit our swimming pool.

"Peter! You did that on purpose!"

"RUFF! RUFF!"

I smiled to myself. My first actual smile in hours. I know my family is crazy. But sometimes crazy is good. Crazy distracts you.

My plan was to record a new TammyBakes video. I hadn't posted in ages. Which was a problem. On the Internet, going dark for too long is a death sentence. You have to keep pumping out content, otherwise people forget you exist.

Also, baking relaxes me. And I needed to relax in the worst way. When I shut my eyes, I could still see Denise's smug face. And then Sheena and Maeve, holding cameras.

Did they really film all my screams?

Maybe the cameras broke, I thought. *Maybe the footage was dark, so they'll have to delete it.*

I tried to relax as I set up my camera. The title of the segment was **BROWNIE BAKING, PART TWO.** I briefly introduced myself, TammyBakes, then dumped my ingredients into a mixing bowl. I used normal amounts this time, with almost no soy sauce.

But for the next part—the mixing—I kind of went overkill.

All my inner frustrations came out.

I started swinging the whisk like a hammer. I beat the bowl with my fists, squeezing my hands through the wet, sticky batter.

I kept pounding and pounding. For hours.

"Take that, Denise." SQUISH! "Did you feel that? Is that what you like?"

"I'M BACK," WHEEZED A VOICE. "Back like a heart attack. *Whoa.*"

I turned around and saw Mom. Beads of sweat dripped down her face from the walk. She stared in shock through her crazy winged glasses.

"Someone call the governor," she teased. "Hurricane Tammy is now a statewide emergency."

I dropped the whisk I was waving around like a chainsaw.

"Sorry, Mom. I got…carried away."

Mom sighed. She made me empty the mixing bowl, then soak my hair in the sink until the brownie mix droplets came out.

"What's for dinner?" I asked.

"We ordered pizza, like, an age ago, duh!" Pete scampered into the kitchen. He stole my whisk from the sink and crammed it into his mouth, like a Popsicle. "Oh wow. What *is* this stuff?"

"Do you like it?" I asked eagerly.

Pete made a face. "It's a crime against chocolate."

I grabbed the whisk away, scowling.

"Hey, no fair! Moommmm! Tammy promised me brownies!"

"Ugh! Fine!" I flung the whisk at him.

I stormed out of the kitchen and into the dining room. Lamps flickered and the chandelier creaked on its chain.

"Everyone alive in there?" Dad teased. He joined Mom and Pete in the dining room. I think Mom had an earthquake joke planned, but a ring at the door interrupted it.

"Perrin's Pizza," drawled a voice.

"Score!" shouted Pete. "I call sausage!"

"I'll be upstairs," I announced. "I'm not hungry."

Mom shot me a look. *"Tammy,"* she said warningly.

"What? I already ate," I lied.

"Will you at least get the door?"

"Will you *please* get the door," Dad corrected. "Pretty please? With a Tammy on top?" He clasped his hands in a prayer pose. "Don't kill us," he whispered.

I laughed without meaning to. "Fine."

I grabbed the doorknob and pulled. Nothing happened. "Unnggh!" I roared in frustration.

"Tammy is maaaad," Pete giggled.

Scowling, I slid the dead bolt aside and flung the door open.

Guess what happened?

A screaming demon attacked me.

11

"OOPS. SORRY ABOUT THAT."

The screaming demon pulled off his mask. He was a high-schooler with earrings and long, greasy hair. The pizza guy. "Some girls paid me five bucks to wear a mask here," he yawned.

My arms wobbled as I lifted the pizzas.

Stay calm, I told myself. *Don't freak out. You're okay.*

I knew Denise had just pranked me again. But knowing the truth couldn't stop me from shaking like a leaf.

"Hey, what's that?" The pizza guy grabbed a narrow black book off the railing. He wiped a bandage off the cover and opened it. *"Ohh sick!"*

A clump of ugly brown slugs splatted onto his shirt! He hopped around, shrieking and gasping, as the slugs slid away.

My face paled. The Halloween cookbook was back!

It was left there for me, I realized. *I was meant to open it. It was supposed to be ME getting slugged.*

I clenched my teeth, feeling my fear slowly twist into anger. I was sick to death of Denise's dumb tricks.

"Nice try," I told the pizza guy. "First the mask. Now the Halloween cookbook. How much is Denise Daddario really paying you? Must be more than five bucks."

"I didn't bring the slug book, I swear. Just the pizzas!" He left the porch like a shot.

BACK INSIDE, I SET the pizzas on the dining room table and turned toward the stairs.

"Sure you aren't hungry?" Mom asked.

I shook my head. "It's been a long day. I need sleep."

"Hey, Tammy's got something!" Pete blurted out. "It's...pizza!"

"No, dork, it isn't." I waved the book at him. "See? Plain old cookbook."

I escaped up the steps.

My bed creaked as I flopped into it, burrowing under the sheets. I looked across to my desk, my small dresser and the orange curtains that covered my window.

All normal. All good.

I rolled onto my back, staring up. I watched the ceiling fan spin. Around and around. I tried to empty my brain of all thought. I never wanted to think of Denise or The Circle Girls ever again.

It didn't work. Ugly thoughts crept back in. My eyes flicked to the Halloween cookbook.

Why did I keep it? Why did I bring it upstairs?

The slugs were gone. I triple-checked.

As for why I kept it, don't laugh. It was because Jake Aberforth gave me it. I knew I told Denise to keep it. I also knew Denise brought it back here tonight, as a prank.

What I didn't know was if Jake was part of her prank. He almost definitely was. But what if he wasn't?

I liked meeting Jake. He was a cool kid. His jokes were funny, most of the time. And he wasn't ugly or anything like that.

Besides, he commented on my TammyBakes video. Maybe. I still wasn't sure if Denise had secretly posted that comment on a separate account. An ugly voice in my head thought she did.

"Of course Denise posted it. Jake is out of your league, Tammy. You aren't famous like Sheena, Maeve and Denise. You're a nobody. No one watches your dumb channel but Pete. So how could someone like Jake leave a comment? Are you just that delusional?"

TWEEP! TWEEP! TWEEP!

Suddenly my phone chimed a news alert. Not just one. A huge wave of alerts. I checked the lockscreen and gasped.

TammyBakes has 7 new comments!

My laptop lit like a flare. From across the room, I saw my "Welcome, TammyBakes" home page flashing like crazy.

I knew it was getting bombarded.

But why? Why was TammyBakes so popular all the sudden?

I rushed to my laptop. My heart raced as I scrolled down the page.

amazing omg what a freak! [#TruthOrScare][#CircleGirls]
– cg4meeee
ded. rip rando's face. gogogo [#TruthOrScare][#CircleGirls]
– sydwhoknows
(=o=) [#TruthOrScare][#IWasHereWhen][#TammyJakes]
– emoji_bot_lover

That's weird, I thought. *#TruthOrScare? What is that?*

A tiny knot formed in my chest. I had a sinking feeling I knew the answer already. My nerves felt electric as I followed the links to the Circle Girls home page.

A large banner filled up the screen.

NEW! The Circle Girls Present: #TruthOrScare.
Episode 1: Sending TammyBakes to the Insane Asylum
[#CircleGirls][#TruthOrScare][#TammyJakes]

I clicked on the video. It was the story of *me.* Me at the lunch table, hearing the tale of Jake Aberforth. Me crossing the haunted woods to the old cabin where Jake lived. Me again, locked in the cabin, screaming my lungs off.

The video had all sorts of close-ups. Someone used filters to alter my face, so when I screamed, it looked like my skin melted off.

But that wasn't the worst part. The worst part came last.

I thought I couldn't get any madder than I already was. But then I saw a different clip of myself. A clip of me talking calmly to Jake. Except some cruel person had used a filter on it, erasing Jake from the video. Now I looked like a maniac! Smiling. Laughing. Giving this huge monologue speech, all alone, in some weird haunted house.

The whole time, Denise's voice gave narrations.

"Will Tammy and Jake find true love? Will Tammy get the psychiatric help she so desperately needs? Tune in next time for a fresh episode of #TruthOrScare! Luv ya! Heart and subscribe!"

I felt sick to my bones. So this was it. The Circle Girls' plan.

I wasn't an idiot. I actually expected something like this. A prank video. With me screaming and being scared by Denise.

But I never expected this level of focus and effort. Everything was close-up and high-definition. There were dozens of angles. Hidden cameras, I guessed. Add in the filters and edits, and it was a masterpiece. I really did look insane.

And you might be thinking, so what, Tammy? Who cares if you look crazy? Didn't your channel get a billion new views? Isn't TammyBakes blowing up, like you wanted? You're a celebrity now. You're famous!

But you're dead wrong. I wasn't famous.

I was *infamous*.

Famous for being a freak.

I felt numb after watching the video. I let out a moan without meaning to. Like my heart was crying in pain.

I stared at the comments. Not one person asked me a question. They typed like I didn't exist. Like I was the butt of some never-ending joke they all shared. Just some weirdo to laugh at.

Until then, I'd never considered the fact I could get famous and hate it. I never knew it could hurt so much. I thought my visitors would all be my fans, looking up to me.

WRONG.

I slammed the laptop screen shut.

I'd never felt so alone.

THAT NIGHT I COULDN'T SLEEP. I kept sneaking peeks at my channel. No miracles. The comments only got worse.

Finally, I unplugged my laptop and hid it under the bed. When I still couldn't sleep, I grabbed the cookbook and flicked through the recipes. I was looking for prank titles, things like that.

But something was different. Something was strange.

The first page looked all right, but for every time I flipped past it, the words blurred together. Pale letters swam on the page. I squinted. I stared. And I couldn't read anything!

"Maybe Denise was right," I mumbled. "Maybe I *have* gone insane."

I fell asleep like that—with my chin on the cookbook, and all these horrible thoughts in my head.

No wonder I had a nightmare.

The worst in my life.

12

THAT NIGHT, IN MY DREAM, I went for a walk. I didn't know where I was walking to, or even what surface I walked on. Dirt maybe? Air? Solid air?

I walked for hours like that. Maybe days.

Finally, I reached my destination.

A door.

The door lay flat on the ground. Steam hissed from the cracks, smelling oddly delicious.

I know.

Without knowing why, I knelt by the door. I started sweeping branches and dust off the top. I did all of this very slowly and carefully, until I could read every word that was scratched on the wood.

CLARISSE'S KITCHEN
ENTER AND DIE

In the dream, my heart skipped a beat.

Clarisse's Kitchen. Wasn't it just like the sign at Jake's cabin? That freaky sign with the stain?

Another shiver ran through me. Should I really go in?

No, Tammy. Leave! Run away!

But the longer I stared, the safer I felt. Sweet-smelling steam filled my lungs. The warm fragrance spread through my body and into my bones, like a web.

Like a wonderful web.

I licked my lips without meaning to. Then I opened the door in one pull.

An old staircase hid underneath.

"Taaaammy," sang a voice from the depths. *"Taaaammy.* Come and visit. Come and enter my kitchen."

My heart trembled. I knew that voice. How did I know it?

"Taaaammy," it repeated.

That's when the dream started changing. Out of nowhere, a strange power seized control of my legs. I let out a gasp as I jerked down the steps, like a puppet. The air was thicker now. Staler. Less fragrant. The mossy stairs creaked, sending chills down my neck.

I didn't want to go down there.

I wanted to stop and go home.

On the last step, I mustered all of my strength. I decided to fight the strange power that was pulling me down.

So I gritted my teeth. Locked my knees together. Refused to go one more inch down those horrible, moss-covered—

"Aaaaaaaahhhh!"

I shrieked as the unknown force dragged me down (down and right, like an "L") and my back slammed on ghostly white tile. Lights flickered. I crawled to my feet, peering round.

A kitchen. Had I entered a kitchen?

"Did you bring it, Tammy? Did you bring my ingredient?"

I gasped and spun around. A gorgeous young chef looked up from the bowl she was stirring. She wore a spotless chef's uniform, with gleaming gold buttons and a tall, furrowed hat. Locks of glistening hair flowed around her thin face. *And her eyes.*

Her crisp, stunning, oven-red eyes.

I instantly knew who she was. "Chef Clarisse."

"The ingredient, child. Where is it?"

"The...ingredient?"

Chef Clarisse frowned. "Come closer, child. Let me see your potential."

I obeyed the command. I moved closer.

Chef Clarisse pointed to the kitchen counter. No. To the narrow black book that lay open across it.

My eyes bulged. *The Halloween cookbook! The Booke of Loste Foodes!*

Her long fingers flicked through the oily black pages. She stopped at the blurriest one, in the back.

"Read," she commanded.

My throat tightened. "I-I can't...it's too blurry."

"Focus, child. This is important."

Chef Clarisse shoved the book at my face. I let out a moan. The sugary-sweet smell was gone, replaced by a thick stench of rot and decay. I started coughing and gasping.

Chef Clarisse pulled *The Booke* away, frowning.

"She is not ready," she sighed. "All this time we have waited, and the girl is not ready." Her scarlet eyes flicked around, landing on a pale figure who stood near the oven. "Grigory! Prepare her!"

"Ysssssss Chfffff."

I shivered as the pale figure—Grigory—came forward. He wore a chef's uniform, too, but he was no Chef Clarisse. Not even close. His huge head was covered in bandages, like a mummy.

A chef mummy.

I watched, horrified, as Grigory opened a drawer and pulled out a butcher's knife. He tipped the seven-inch blade toward his face.

No. His eye. *His single blue eye.*

The other eye was trapped behind bandages.

I felt chills as he twisted the knife, very slowly, until the tip pointed at my face.

Please, no, I thought crazily. *Not me…not my eye…*

Grigory scraped out a laugh. He motioned to a nearby mixing bowl, as if he wanted to plop my eye in it.

It was the scariest situation I'd ever faced in my life. The dream felt so real. So intense. I backed toward the wall, twisting and writhing.

Grigory stalked forward. There was something familiar about his weird walk. What was it? The question made me quake even more.

"Noooo," I moaned. "Please…not my eye…"

The butcher's knife flashed as it fell toward my face.

13

I WOKE UP IN A FEVER. Fear clogged my throat as I struggled to breathe.

The oven? Was I trapped in the oven?

I jerked my head up and stared.

No. I was fine. I was safe in my room.

"Oh thank God." I took deep, calming breaths. "Just a dream. Just a dream."

Still shaking, I stripped the sheets off my bed and changed clothes. But even in shorts and a tank I felt sweaty.

Why was I sweaty?

I pulled the curtains apart. Cold wind rushed my face as I opened the window. Crickets chirped. Frogs croaked beneath the silver full moon.

6:02, said the clock.

I crawled back in bed. I tried to sleep, but whenever I closed my eyes, I saw Grigory, pointing his knife at me.

It all felt so real. A real knife. A real mummy.

But it wasn't real, I told myself. *It was a nightmare. There is no Chef Clarisse and no mummy chef.*

So how come the chills wouldn't stop?

Still trembling, still hot, I decided to stay awake for a while. It was Saturday, right? No school. I knew I could take an afternoon nap if I wanted.

I closed *The Booke of Loste Foodes* and stashed it under my bed, with my laptop. I felt instantly better. Just seeing *The Booke* made me scowl.

I knew Denise was behind it. It fit her sick personality. I fumed at the thought she was *still* pranking me, even in dreams.

I hid my phone away, too. I didn't want to see the alerts. I knew TammyBakes would have even more comments now.

Prank comments.

Bad comments.

The thought of reading them twisted my stomach.

I left my bedroom and tiptoed into the hall. Since I couldn't sleep, there was one thing I could try. One thing that always relaxed me.

Being a chef. Cooking breakfast.

I ALMOST DIDN'T MAKE IT downstairs. The silent walk down was too freaky. Too much like the stairs in my dream. Heart thudding, I held my breath till the bottom, then found myself tiptoeing right, toward the kitchen. That's when I froze up completely.

It was the exact same right turn. The exact same dark kitchen.

My jaw dropped and my legs turned to stone. I had no idea what had happened.

Another dream? Was I dreaming?

No. Impossible.

Right?

Slowly, silently, I unfroze my legs and inched forward. I reached a shivering hand for the light switch.

"Please, please don't be dreaming," I begged.

CLICK!

Yellow light flooded the room.

Oh thank God.

No Chef Clarisse. No cookbook. No mummy.

Everything looked normal and clean. I choked out the breath I was holding. Then I inhaled again, feeling calmer already.

For breakfast, my plan was ambitious. French toast. Pancakes. Half a carton of eggs (over easy). I knew my behavior last night wasn't great. I'd stomped around, acting rude and insane.

I didn't want to act insane anymore. I wanted to be Nice Tammy—a warm summer breeze—and cook a huge breakfast for Mom, Dad and Pete.

For me, too. I was *starving*.

I crossed the kitchen, gathering pots, pans and plates. If I focused, I thought I could just barely cook everything on my list, even though my thoughts were full of hate and revenge.

And Denise. Dumb Denise.

"Just ignore her," I told myself. "Focus on food."

And I tried to. I really did.

I turned the stove on. I set my pots and plates on the counter, ignoring the hungry growl in my stomach. But when it came time to fetch my ingredients, I opened the cupboard and—

Crud.

"Nothing's here. It's all gone!"

I couldn't believe it. Had I really used all Mom's ingredients up? *In one day?* Ugh. I really had been a Hurricane Tammy.

My stomach growled again.

Eggs. Did we even have eggs?

No.

The only food was a box of cold pizza that sat on the counter. I stared at it. I didn't want to eat it. No way. But then again, after skipping dinner last night...

I suddenly lunged for the box. Flipped it open.

Two slices.

But as I reached for a slice, my hand froze. The pizza toppings were pepperoni with red peppers and lettuce— and eyeballs.

Whole eyeballs.

14

I SCREAMED AND THREW THE box at the ceiling. The greasy lid cracked as cold pizza plunged toward my head. I squealed and leapt backward.

SPLAT! SPLAT! SPLAT!

"Phew. That was close."

I stared at the cheese-covered spot I'd just left.

The eyeball? Where was the eyeball?

One of the toppings jerked forward. I watched it roll sideways, past the pizza, then scuttle away on six legs.

"Ohh sick!" I cried.

Not an eyeball. A cockroach!

It slipped through a crack in the door.

I spent the next hour cleaning the kitchen. I wrapped the pizza in napkins, flinging it into the trash. I scrubbed the grease away. Scrubbed the sink. Scrubbed the floor again. I was so busy, I barely noticed the sun as it crept in the window.

"Tammy, whoa. What's for breakfast?"

My brother Pete wandered in. He looked like a wild animal. He was shirtless, with crazy bed hair and baseball pants rolled to his knees.

"No breakfast," I sighed. "We're all out of food."

"Liar." Pete started digging around in the trash. He found a pizza slice instantly.

"A cockroach was in that," I warned.

Pete rolled his eyes. He took a big bite, then opened his mouth extra wide, so I could watch as he chewed it.

"Ugh. You're disgusting." I turned to leave, but out of nowhere, a lightning bolt struck me. A super genius idea. I whipped around, pointing at Pete's open mouth.

"The cockroach!" I gasped. "I can see its antennae!"

"Whaaaa—?!" Pete froze in mid-chew. His face turned pea-green as he raced to the sink, making choking sounds. I watched him bury his face in the faucet.

"Gotcha," I said.

I laughed all the way back to my bedroom. I was so happy. So impressed with my genius. Guess why?

I suddenly knew how to get my revenge on Denise.

MOM AND DAD WERE both up when I skipped down the stairs, fully dressed. "I'm going to the store," I announced.

"Blue skies and sunny," Mom smirked.

Dad grinned at the cookbook I carried. "Any winners, kiddo?"

"A couple, I guess." I paused at the door, hesitating. "Mom? Dad?" I said warily. "Do either of you know a place that sells...slugs?"

"Excuse me?"

"Slugs. Wild slugs. Do shops sell them?"

"Tammy, if this is for one of your recipes—"

"It isn't," I lied. "I will never, ever serve you a slug." *Probably.*

Mom and Dad traded 'Tammy is weird' looks and shrugged. Finally, Mom reached into her purse and gave me a short grocery list, plus forty dollars in cash.

"Don't forget Cheetos," said Dad, as I slipped out the door.

Out in the garage, I strapped the wire luggage rack to my bike. As I rolled down the driveway, I felt amazing. Full of crackling energy.

I burst out laughing as I turned onto Main Street.

My plan was so perfect. So good.

I was going to bake the Chiller Cookies from Denise's dumb cookbook. Somehow, I was going to trick her into eating one.

On camera.

Earlier, when I'd inspected the recipe, I decided the steps were probably real. I'd baked tons of normal cookies before. The Halloween ingredients were mostly the same. Except for one, of course.

FINAL INGREDIENT ALERT! SLUGS (WILD, 32CT.)

My eyes squinted. Could I do it? Could I really put slugs in a mixing bowl? Roll them each into balls? Slide the balls in the oven, like cookies? Like food?

Yes.

For Denise Daddario, yes.

Except, where was I going to find slugs? How would I convince Denise to eat slug-covered cookies?

I didn't know yet. So far, all I had was my starting point. I was going to launch my own web series, starring Denise and the Circle Girls. My plan was to film every step of my work. Buying ingredients. Mixing them in a bowl. Sneakily plopping in slugs.

For my grand finale, I would film Denise with her mouth full of slugs. A close-up shot. High-definition.

I wanted to record the exact moment her teeth bit the slug. The exact second her tongue felt that juicy slug taste. If she screamed, I'd be recording that, too. Maybe later I'd add a face-melt effect, just for fun.

Imagine the response that would get on my Tam-myBakes channel—*which was packed full of Circle Girls viewers.*

Wouldn't they just freak? Wouldn't everyone copy the link?

Boom! Viral video.

It was the perfect revenge.

The perfect way to get famous.

"Whoaaa!" I cried out, as my handlebars shook unexpectedly. An eerie crunch underneath my front tire jerked me back to reality.

I looked around frantically.

Dirt. Gravel. Trees.

What was going on? Where was Main Street?

Why was THE FOREST TRAIL underneath me?

My tires skidded crazily as I slammed on the brakes. I shut my eyes, feeling the handlebars jerk toward a—

THUMP!

I hit the tree at full speed. Twigs snapped as I smashed to the dirt, dragging gravel and leaves. My heart thumped like a jack hammer.

Alone. I was alone in the haunted forest.

I gasped as a cluster of leaves loudly shook. Was someone out there? Was someone watching me?

The leaves shook again. I peered closer. My heart was speeding out of control when I saw it. A single blue eye, staring out of the trees.

Only one.

15

THE EYE BLINKED AND disappeared, leaving a person-sized gap in the branches. I was even more shocked to see Jake's cabin between the bent leaves.

Was it really that close?

Hadn't I just barely entered the trail?

"Jake!" I called suddenly. "Jake Aberforth! Are you out there?"

The wind whistled. I heard a faint scraping noise. Something was clawing its way up a tree. My heart skipped, even though I knew I was safe.

"A squirrel. Just a squirrel on a branch."

I peered closer. *The squirrel had one eye.* There was a pink scar where its second eye should have been.

My heart thumped. As I stared, a second one-eyed squirrel scurried by. Then a third.

A fourth.

A fifth.

A sixth.

When my count reached thirteen, *thirteen one-eyed squirrels*, I finally let out the scream that was building inside of me.

"AaaaaAAaaaaAAAAAaaaaaahhhhh!"

The one-eyed squirrels skipped away.

A second later, I grabbed my bike and fled, too.

"IS EVERYTHING ALL RIGHT, dear? You look spooked."

"The milk aisle was a little chilly, that's all," I told the cashier.

I tried to relax as she rang up my items. This was supposed to be my big moment. The opening scene of my video. But how could I film myself buying groceries when I was still shaking like a leaf?

"Yo, TammyBakes!" cried a voice in the parking lot.

"Aaaaahhh!" another person fake-screamed.

Five boys in baseball pants were doubled up, laughing. I scowled as their leader, the king of the dorks, strutted forward.

"Hey Tammy, nice video!" Pete cackled. He seized my bike rack and started shaking it. *It's aaaliiive! The food is aaaaaaaliiive!*

"Stop that!" I snapped. "You'll crack the eggs!"

"Those poor eggs. Little do they know, they're about to be part of the grossest dessert in the galaxy."

"Is it true?" said a boy in a Mets shirt. "Are you the real TammyBakes?"

"Ask her to scream," hissed a Diamondback.

"Careful," Pete warned. "Tammy's screaming could melt your face off!"

More laughter. I felt my cheeks redden. Since when was I a punching bag for ten-year-olds?

"Hilarious, Pete, very funny." I swept past him, addressing his weird little gang. "Did Pete tell you he ate cockroach pizza for breakfast?"

The boys blinked.

"C-Cockroach? You ate one?"

"That true?"

Pete whirled on them, releasing a hideous burp. "Rawwwr! Roach breath!" He flashed an evil grin as they staggered away.

"TammyBakes!" whooped the boys as they left.

I watched them go with a scowl.

"Maybe I'll take revenge on you, too," I muttered under my breath.

"And...cut!" A giggling voice shouted. I let out a groan as Sheena, Maeve and Denise stepped out of hiding. Their cell phone screens flashed as they frantically swiped.

"I used zoom. Did you zoom, Maeve?"

"Duh. And I know just the right filter!"

My eyes popped. I almost couldn't believe it. "Y-You were filming me?"

The Circle Girls huddled up, talking in low, urgent voices.

"Ask her."

"No, you ask her."

"You're such wimps, do you know that?"

Denise pulled away from them, her green eyes flashing like emeralds as she strutted up to me. "Hey Taffy. I mean, Tammy. It's Tammy, right?"

I didn't answer.

"Well, we were just wondering if you would help us again. It's for #TruthOrScare. Have you seen it?"

I didn't answer again.

"You see, we're doing a follow-up video. Behind the scenes stuff. It's really popular right now."

"I bet it is," I mumbled.

"Basically, we want to film a new scene with you. A *specific* scene. We want to hear all about Jake. As much as you know."

I blinked. "Huh? Didn't you cut Jake out of the video? You made me look completely insane. Like a freak!"

Sheena and Maeve burst out laughing. Denise shushed them, but she was half-laughing too.

"About that," said Denise. "Jake begged us not to put him on camera. So, um, we couldn't refuse him. But we can still tell *your* side of the story, Tammy. I think viewers would be fascinated to hear it."

I tried not to groan.

Did I believe a word of this garbage? No. Of course not. But I also realized this was my chance. Another film shoot. Another opportunity to hang out with the Circle Girls—*and to bring my special snack along.*

"When?" I said finally.

"Tonight," said Denise. "We're having a birthday sleepover at Sheena's. We plan to film the whole night."

The whole night?

"No need to bring a gift, Tammy. Just your scream. Haha."

"Um, what time?"

"Pick you up around five."

I did a rough calculation. It was eleven o'clock now. So six hours. Could I have the Chiller Cookies prepared in six hours? My original plan was to wait until Monday and bring them to school. That left me plenty of time to practice the recipe. I was worried the slugs might look too obvious once the cookies were baked.

On the other hand, if I brought Chiller Cookies to Sheena McAfee's mansion tonight…if I pranked Denise on home turf, at the famous Circle Girls hangout…

My heart quickened.

Could it work? What if something went wrong?

Denise had pranked me before, and I *knew* she would try it again. I was walking into a trap if I went to Sheena McAfee's party tonight.

I bit my lip, thinking hard. Was there a way I could ruin Denise's prank? What if I dodged it, then pulled off my own prank instead? Was it possible? Was I that daring?

"Excellent!" Denise's voice interrupted. "See you at five, Tammy!"

"Um, okay," I heard myself mumble.

"By the way," Denise added. "Tonight's video is actually a live stream. Thousands of people will be watching you, so dress to impress, okay?"

Denise giggled as she, Maeve and Sheena strode off.

Leaving me standing there. Frozen in shock.

A live stream? In front of THOUSANDS of people?

My heart shivered. What had I done? What had I just agreed to?

16

I WASN'T SMILING ANYMORE as I turned onto Main Street. I felt frazzled.

The live stream changed everything.

"It's fine," I tried telling myself. "Launching a web series was too complicated, anyway. One, you never shot any scenes for it. Two, it takes *forever*. Three, isn't a live stream much faster?"

I nodded along to my thoughts.

"When you're live, there are no scripts to write. No tricky edits. So what if you're scared to death of embarrassing yourself in front of thousands of people. Just smile and hand out your cookies. That's it."

Whether I believed that or not, it still left one problem.

The slugs.

For the next thirty minutes, I rode my bike everywhere. I checked the town pond. I flipped over rocks in a stream bed. Finally, I walked into Scales 'n' Tails, our town pet shop, babbling nonsense at the clerk by the reptile tanks.

"Slugs?" said the clerk. "Wow, that's awesome. How cool! Let me guess. You have some hungry chameleons at home?"

"Well, actually—"

"Chameleons do love their slugs! They're carnivores, so they'll munch almost anything wiggly. Worms. Ants. Baby toads."

The clerk's eyes strayed to the chameleons' tank, as if remembering all the exotic creatures she'd fed them.

"At this shop, however, we only sell crickets. We don't sell the rest." The clerk looked up at me. "Can I interest you in a bag of live crickets?"

AN HOUR LATER, I set the crickets on top of the kitchen counter. They were alive, all right. They wouldn't stop hopping inside of the bag.

"Don't come in," I warned Mom and Dad. "This is a serious operation."

"Partly cloudy, with a chance of sweets," Mom predicted.

Dad chuckled. "Just remember, kiddo, we need the kitchen for dinner."

"That's fine. I might not be home tonight, anyway."

I explained about Sheena's birthday party. My parents beamed in surprise. They seemed pretty impressed.

"The McAfee mansion? Wow!"

"Sure you don't need a ride?"

"I'll be fine. Someone's picking me up."

Five minutes later, I finally shook off their questions and got to work. I laid *The Booke of Loste Foodes* on the stove, near the oven. I wanted a close-up view of the recipe.

I was very excited. I knew using crickets instead of slugs was a risk. Not every ingredient can be easily substituted. But how bad could it be? Wasn't one creepy-crawly just as gross as the next?

Time flew. Before long, the introductory steps were complete. I beamed as I switched on my camera. I'd reached the critical point: adding crickets.

Filming this step was extremely important. I needed proof that my cookies were gross, in case the Circle Girls tried denying it later.

"These are the crickets," I announced. "See them hopping?"

I waved the bag around. I hadn't opened it yet. I was too worried the crickets would escape. If they did, how would I catch them? How would I explain myself then?

I pictured myself rushing around, trying to scoop up the crickets.

"Is everything all right?" Mom would ask. *"I hear rumbles."*

"That isn't thunder, Mom. It's a cricket stampede."

Ugh. Can you imagine?

Well, what actually happened was, I opened the bag and the crickets lay still.

They were dead. Suffocated.

I felt suddenly sick. I'd never really considered the fate of the crickets. Okay, fine. I was going to drown them in cookie dough, then put that dough in the oven.

But I didn't realize…I didn't stop and think…

I shivered as I lifted the cricket bag. The dead crickets tumbled and rolled. I didn't wink for the camera, like I planned. I forgot I was even filming a scene as I tipped the bag toward the mixing bowl.

An icy chill crept down my throat, past my quivering cheeks, as an unknown voice whispered, *"I wouldn't do that if I were you. I wouldn't alter Mom's recipe."*

I looked around. "Who said that?"

"Never mess with a classic, Tammy. Bad things could happen."

I spun around in a circle, my eyes frantic.

"W-Who's there?" I cried. "What do you want?"

"Reveeennnngge," the voice cackled.

I suddenly felt my eyes start to itch. A rotten smell stabbed my nose as I spun around and saw—

"Smoke!"

Waves of oily black smoke, blasting out of the oven.

B-But the oven was empty! H-How could it smoke?

With a nasty jolt, I realized my legs were frozen. I was pinned to the spot. Shaking in fear as the smoke alarm shrieked.

BZZZ!!! BZZZ!!! BZZZ!!!

"Tammy!" shrieked a voice. *"TAMMY!"*

Footsteps crashed down the hall.

"D-Don't come any closer," I warned. "S-Stop. P-Please."

I closed my eyes. I was delirious. Choking and gasping, as Dad grabbed my hips from behind, dragging me out of the smoke.

17

WHEN I CAME TO, Mom was squeezing my hand. We were huddled outside, watching Dad as he trudged through the house.

"I found it. I found the culprit."

When Dad reappeared, he was holding a narrow black book.

"M-My cookbook?" I spluttered. "My cookbook caused the smoke?"

"Huh? No, of course not." Dad flipped me the cookbook. "Thought you might want it back. Actually, the source of the smoke was the oven."

The oven?

My face paled. "There was nothing in it, Dad. I swear!"

Dad frowned at me. "You've been using that oven nonstop without cleaning it. Can't do that, kiddo. We're lucky the grease fire burned itself out. It should be safe now. But you need to be more careful in the future, okay? Cooking is a big responsibility."

I hung my head. "Can I still use the oven?"

Mom and Dad traded looks. "Yes."

I raced to the door.

"After you've cleaned out the swimming pool."

My feet slid to a halt. "But that's Pete's chore, not mine!"

"Pete didn't smoke up the house," Dad replied.

"A GREASE FIRE," I said aloud. "Just a grease fire. An accident."

But then whose voice did I hear? Who warned me not to alter the recipe? Was it the smoke? Did the smoke somehow mess with my head?

"Unnngh!" I clenched my teeth, swinging the pool skimmer like a battle axe. I watched it shudder and crash through the waves. My anger was surging up again. Why was everything so hard today?

I decided the universe wasn't helping me, after all. It kept deliberately messing things up.

The sky trembled as the first raindrops rippled the swimming pool.

"Perfect," I growled. "Just what I needed."

I swung the skimmer again. It jerked left and jammed itself into the pool filter. I pulled on it angrily. Crazily.

"Arrgh! Why won't anyone help me!"

"I already did."

A voice? Was that a voice? I fell silent, listening to the clouds as they rumbled. Then suddenly I did hear a voice.

"HOME! I AM HOME! I AM HOME!"

A distant door slammed as Pete trampled into the house. I let out a groan. Then I instantly tripled my cleaning speed. The last thing I needed was Pete catching me doing chores for him.

I crossed the patio and knelt beside the pool filter. I slipped my hand through the lid, then gasped as I opened it.

Slugs. Tons of slugs!

A wave of horror shot through me.

"Hang on," I said suddenly. "Aren't these the same slugs Denise pranked me with?" I leaned closer. Had they crawled off the porch? Did they plop themselves into the pool overnight?

A smile stretched across my lips. "Thank you, universe," I said. "And thank you, Denise. This is perfect!"

I put the skimmer away, rushed inside and came back with a giant glass jar. I tossed the dead crickets into the trash, along with the muck from the filter. Well, *most* of it.

"Slugs," I whispered. "Wild. Thirty-two."

Grinning, I scooped their fat bodies into the jar.

I had just what I needed.

A SHORT WHILE LATER…

THUMP!

The oven door slammed on my cookie balls. My skin prickled as I peered through the glass. I imagined all the wonderful things I would do once my cookies were baked. My top secret, slug-covered cookies.

Sixteen minutes, said the timer.

Crisp lightning lit up the house. I paced around, feeling more and more anxious. The halls were quiet. Mom, Dad and Pete were still napping. For a split second, I thought about joining them. I hadn't slept since forever. My eyes drooped as I swayed toward the last open seat on the—

Stop.

Visions of Chef Clarisse and the mummy chef jerked me awake. I stopped short, suddenly shaking all over. A nightmare was the last thing I needed. I decided to go upstairs to shower and change. To get myself ready for Sheena's.

"This is going to be a great night," I tried telling myself.

"Or a trainwreck," said the voice in my head.

18

THE TIMER RANG OFF while I was still getting dressed.

Arrrgh! No time! No time!

I pulled my sweatshirt on backwards, then forwards, then raced down the steps. I couldn't believe how careless I'd been. How distracted! At the end of the stairs, I swerved right, toward the kitchen—and gasped.

"Moooomm! W-What are you doing? Don't touch that!"

My eyes stretched as Mom pulled my cookie tray out of the oven. She placed it gently on the kitchen counter, taking big sniffs of slug cookie air.

Oh no, I thought. Oh-no, oh-no, oh-no.

Did she smell the slugs? Could she tell what I did?

"COOKIES!" My brother Pete darted into the kitchen.

"Nooo!" I squeaked. "Stop! Pete—"

Time slowed to a crawl as Pete scooped a Chiller Cookie into his palm. He raised it to his lips. Opened wide.

CRRRNNNCH!

One of the slugs loudly crunched as he chomped it in half.

I let out a moan. My entire life flashed before my eyes.

Pete collapsing onto the floor.

Pete being airlifted to the hospital.

Pete, lying dead, as a policewoman slapped me in hand-cuffs.

I watched the cookie dissolve in Pete's mouth. He swallowed hard. I could barely imagine the grossness he felt. The slow creep of slug down his throat. He grunted and opened his eyes.

"W-Where did you get these?" Pete spluttered. "They're...GREAT!"

Mom beamed in surprise. "Tammy made them."

"Don't lie," Pete demanded. "You bought these."

Two more cookies disappeared before Mom finally stopped him from eating.

To say I was shocked is an understatement. I had no idea what had happened. Was Pete pranking me? No. Impossible. I saw the cookie myself. At least one of those slugs cracked in half!

So what happened? Did Pete actually like eating slugs?

My stomach twisted. It was disgusting to think about.

I felt a bump as Mom pressed the cookie tray into my chest.

"You should box these up, Tammy. Before Tsunami Pete sweeps them away."

I nodded limply. My thoughts were a mess.

Maybe Pete didn't eat a slug, I reasoned. Maybe he ate the only three cookies without them, and that's why he didn't react.

But hadn't I seen the slug? Hadn't it crunched in Pete's teeth?

You don't know what you saw, Tammy. It could've been baking flour or a clump of butter. You've never made Chiller Cookies before. How could you know what an oven-baked slug even looks like?

HNNNK!! HNNNK!!

My thoughts were interrupted by a loud honk from the driveway.

"Tammy?" Dad said suspiciously. "Did you join the mob recently? Did you win a Grammy award without telling us?"

I followed Dad's eyes to the window. A pearly-white vehicle took up all of our driveway and half of the street.

My jaw dropped.

A stretch Hummer.

19

I SAT ALONE IN THE Hummer, enjoying the spacious rear cabin. The panels were genuine gold. Leather seats traced the walls in an elegant loop, enough to fit dozens of people.

So where were they?

"Are you sure no one else is coming?" I asked Sheena's driver, the smiling old man from before. He shrugged as we rolled up the street.

I opened one of the free water bottles, took a sip, and repeated the question. I leaned my face all the way forward this time, just to make sure the driver could—

THUMP!

A glass shield instantly sprang up between us. The cabin doors clicked and locked as thick webbing blackened the windows. Except for a strange pinhole light, I was plunged into darkness.

Oh God.

"Hey! What did you—WHOAAA!"

I screamed as the Hummer veered left—and kept veering. Our huge tires screeched. We were spinning out of control. Round and round.

My heart pounded out of my chest. A strange object started banging the windows. I heard horrible clicking and scrapes as the Hummer swerved onto rougher terrain, shaking like a giant massage chair.

"Tree!" shrieked the driver. "Not the forest trail! Noooo!"

THE FOREST TRAIL?

Panicked, I slammed my fists on the glass shield dividing us. "Turn around! Turn around!"

"Ow! You're hurting me!" the driver squealed.

"Huh?" I gasped. "Me?"

"MEEEE!!!" rasped a shocking third voice. Terrified, I flung myself back. I gripped the black leather seats as the driver sped up. We swung violently left and violently right, our tires screeching like apes, until my last living nerve snapped in half.

I couldn't take it any longer.

"AaaaAAhhhhhh!" I screamed. "AAAaaaaAHHHH!"

I was still screaming when the stretch Hummer slid to a stop. Daylight flooded the cabin as a side door flew open.

"Gotcha, Tammy."

Denise Daddario leered through the gap. Behind her, Sheena McAfee and Maeve Sammler came sprinting out of the mansion.

"It worked! It perfectly worked!"

"A live broadcast from inside the Hummer!"

I stared out the window, at the McAfee's massive stone driveway. It traced a full loop, with thick trees on each bend and a portion of river rocks filling the middle. Denise giggled as a voice echoed out of her cell phone ("MEEEE!!!").

My face reddened. Another prank! The stretch Hummer had scraped past the trees, then spun itself onto the river rocks. The pinhole light was a live-streaming camera.

My blood boiled. I glared at Sheena's driver, the smiling old man.

"Jus' followin' orders," he said. "Nothin' personal."

"Yeah. Whatever." I squeezed my cookie case until the lid almost cracked.

I should have known, I thought. I should have predicted this.

As I walked toward the mansion, my last ounce of pity and doubt seeped away. All I felt now was anger.

Anger and hate.

Stupid Denise. Stupid Circle Girls.

They were going to pay.

20

I FOLLOWED SHEENA, Maeve and Denise through a set of polished oak doors and into the mansion.

"Thanks, Daddy, for buying the Hummer!"

Sheena rushed up to a short, balding man, sweeping him into a hug.

"It's only a rental," said Mr. McAfee.

Sheena shot him a glare, squeezing harder.

"I'll call the dealership—ask for—a price," he choked.

Sheena beamed and released him.

Did I mention the McAfee's house was enormous? It took forever to reach the sliding glass door to the patio.

"Are we really filming outside?" I asked.

"No, silly. At Sheena's."

Denise pointed to what I thought at first was a whole different property.

"You have a house? Your own house?"

"Technically it's the guest house," said Maeve.

"No, *Maeve*, it's mine," Sheena snapped. "Daddy said so."

"Quiet," hissed Denise. "Someone's coming. It's *her*."

Mrs. McAfee strolled into view. She looked like an older, peppier Sheena. Her bracelets were golden, not silver, and she bounced on her heels as she swanned across the patio.

Sheena, Maeve and Denise turned away, completely ignoring her. The move caught me by surprise. Unsure what to do, I glanced from the girls to Mrs. McAfee—then to Mrs. McAfee's pink logo t-shirt.

It felt like a lightning bolt smashed on my brain.

"Clarisse's Kitchen?" I read aloud.

"See, I knew I wasn't invisible!" Mrs. McAfee beamed. "Old shirt, old memories, doll. Do you recognize it?"

I struggled to speak.

"I'm not surprised if you do," she went on. "Clarisse's Kitchen was extremely well-liked. Chef Clarisse was unstoppable. A rising star. Such a shame how it ended. Her poor son…" Mrs. McAfee's voice trailed away.

My jaw dropped. Chef Clarisse? Was it the same Chef Clarisse?

She was famous?

"Mom, stop hogging my friends!" Sheena stomped up to us, grabbing my hand and dragging me across the patio.

"Bye, girls!" Mrs. McAfee waved with her wine glass. "Have fun tonight!"

No one breathed a word until we entered the guest house.

"That was close," Sheena gasped.

"Too close," said Denise.

"My cookies!" I cried suddenly. "I left them out on the patio!"

Denise laughed as she bolted the door.

"I think you can go an hour without eating, Tammy."

"She could go longer than that," Sheena whispered.

The Circle Girls giggled.

WHAT'S THE DIFFERENCE between an Apple Store and Sheena McAfee's guest house? Not a lot. Looking round, I counted six huge TVs. Ten laptops. Enough tangled wire to give a Martian free Internet. Almost every piece of hardware lay sideways or upside down as Maeve rushed around, trying to fix things.

"Daddy lent me this stuff," Sheena bragged. "It's cutting edge Hollywood."

Denise flung herself into a leather computer chair, nearly clipping Maeve's feet as she rolled.

"Watch it, Maeve!"

"Sorry, sorry!"

Denise turned to me. "This is where we film," she said, pointing to a spot in the corner. I looked up and saw the famous Circle Girls banner. It drooped slightly, above the three famous bean bags (gold, silver, bronze) and the logo dance mat that looked so incredibly cool on the Internet.

"It's smaller than I expected," I blurted out.

Denise smirked. "Sometimes the truth is a shock, isn't it?"

My eyes scrunched. What did *that* mean?

Before I could answer, the storm arrived. Thunder boomed as rain hit the house in thick sheets. I stared out the window, at the soaking wet patio.

My poor cookies.

Denise shoved me into a chair next to Sheena's third laptop. "Wait here, Tammy. We're almost ready."

My heart thumped as loud as the raindrops.

"Aren't you hungry?" I said desperately. "I brought cookies. If you don't mind, I'll step out and—"

"Ew, no. Cookies make you fat, Tammy."

"Just try it. Try one."

"Never in a billion years. Gross."

My heart sank. What was I going to do now?

"Got it!" Maeve whooped. She pointed to one of Sheena's TVs. A short video played on a loop. It was a clip of me, screaming like a wild animal inside of the Hummer. Rude comments scrolled down the side.

So it really was a live broadcast...

Suddenly the screen shifted. I felt a flood of relief as my screaming face disappeared—then a flood of horror, pure horror, as I noticed the face that replaced it.

Me again. Current me.

I saw my own eyes as they bulged with surprise.

"Ready for your live interview, Tammy?"

Denise tapped the laptop. Its pinhole light switched to red, for record.

Fzzzz! It abruptly clicked off.

"Ugh, it stopped streaming!" Denise groaned.

Sheena cursed. "It's the storm! The stupid rain blocks the Wi-Fi!"

"That isn't how Wi-Fi works," Maeve explained.

"Then FIX IT, Maeve!"

Maeve dropped to her knees, making swishing sounds as she checked on the wires. Sheena clinked her bracelets impatiently, while Denise muttered "Hurry!" and "I don't have all day."

None of them noticed the screen when it shifted again. Someone's old yearbook photo popped into view. Class of 2000, it said, beneath an image of a boy with wavy brown hair and piercing blue eyes.

My eyes widened. *"Jake?"* I gasped. *"Jake Aberforth?"*

A series of newspaper clippings scrolled down the screen. The black-and-white scans were so faint, they almost looked prehistoric.

"Beloved Chef Clarisse and Son, Jake, Feared Dead."
"Clarisse's Kitchen Disaster! Two missing."
"Jake Aberforth, In Memoriam. 1986-1998."

A slideshow. The pictures and text kept repeating. Leaving me breathless.

This can't be right, I thought. *Someone has to have faked this.*

Hadn't I just spoken with Jake at the cabin?

"Maeve, you idiot!" cried Denise, finally spotting the screen. "You put the slideshow up early! I can't *believe* it. Tammy wasn't supposed to see this until after the interview! Now she won't lie about meeting Jake Aberforth. She won't look insane. She'll know that we know Jake is dead."

My blood chilled. What was going on?

Jake was dead?

21

NO. NO WAY. OF COURSE not.

I gritted my teeth. I suddenly saw through Denise's dumb plan.

"I know what you're up to," I snapped. "You want to trick me into believing Jake Aberforth died—that the boy I met was actually, what, his ghost or something? Wow. That's why you erased Jake from our video, isn't it?"

"Those are real newspaper clippings," Sheena insisted. "I did the microfilm scans in the library, all by myself."

"Ahem."

"Quiet, Maeve. You know what I meant."

BOOOOMMMMM!!!

A thunderclap ripped through the house. Lamps clicked. Screens fizzled. The cute, light-blue eyes in Jake's photograph flickered and died, along with the rest of our lights.

"Aww man! A blackout!"

"Let's go," Sheena hissed. "The mansion has battery backup."

"What about Tammy?"

"Leave her. Maybe Jake will come visit!"

The sliding door opened and closed as three cell phone lights bobbed out of view, across the soaking wet patio. I slumped in my seat.

Those newspaper clippings didn't look fake, said a voice in my head.

I didn't want to believe it. I wanted to believe Sheena, Maeve and Denise could pull off a convincing fake newspaper, complete with faded text and smears from the scanner.

But it seemed really unlikely.

Weren't these the geniuses who stuffed a cabin with lame Halloween junk? They weren't sneaky at all. No way could they fake a whole newspaper.

I sank to the floor, hugging my knees. Memories flashed through my brain, seeming to light up the darkness.

The rusty sign outside Jake's house. Mrs. McAfee's logo t-shirt. The nightmare kitchen I dreamed about. They all said one thing. *Clarisse's Kitchen.*

I thought back to the voice that I'd heard in the kitchen. "I wouldn't do that if I were you. I wouldn't alter Mom's recipe."

MOM'S recipe.

Did that mean Chef Clarisse's recipe? Clarisse Aberforth? Could the raspy voice have belonged to her son, Jake?

I shuddered as I imagined Jake—sweet, blue-eyed Jake—as Chef Clarisse's mummy assistant, raising a knife to his eye patch.

Wait. Hadn't Chef Clarisse called the mummy chef by a different name? Grigory? Did that mean Jake was still around? Still alive?

Hang on. The Jake who I met was only twelve or thirteen. He looked exactly like his yearbook photo. Exactly.

But that photo was twenty years old!

My brain finally broke. I let out a horrified moan.

"Lies," I muttered. It's all lies. It's all part of the prank."

I couldn't believe Jake Aberforth was a missing person from twenty years ago. The boy I met must be someone else. Not Jake. One of Denise's friends, just pretending.

Yes, I thought. Yes. It makes sense!

The whole night was a setup. It was just like I said. The Circle Girls wanted me to think I'd been talking out loud to a ghost.

"Just a prank," I whispered. "Just a prank. Just a prank."

I was still whispering, still crazily praying to God, when the lights came on. Laptops whirred and rebooted. Within moments, I found myself staring at a screen that said, "Launch Live Recording? Yes / No."

How ironic, right?

The door thumped as Sheena, Maeve and Denise rushed inside.

"Boo!" they cried. "It's me, Jake!"

I did my best to ignore their shrill laughter. But I still had one question. One thing that I desperately needed to ask.

"Who was the boy who played Jake?" I demanded. "The boy you dressed up to look exactly like Jake Aberforth's yearbook photo from twenty years ago? You almost had me fooled, guys. You really put a lot of effort into getting the look right."

The Circle Girls blinked at me. "Huh?"

"The boy from the cabin," I said. "The boy pretending to be Jake."

"You don't have to lie anymore," said Denise. "The prank is over. We caught you lying and punished you. Now everyone knows you're a freak."

"I am not!" My face reddened. "I saw a boy in that cabin. You put him there!"

"It was probably Jake's ghost," Maeve said quietly.

"A ghost!?" Sheena squeaked. "From the forest trail?"

Denise rolled her eyes. "Ghosts aren't real, Sheena. I only said that before to prank Tammy."

"If ghosts are real, they would definitely live in that cabin," Maeve said. "It's too creepy."

"Maybe Tammy should go and live there. She could feed Jake one of her freaky desserts." Denise's eyes glittered. "Oh my God, how sick was that cookbook? Remember?"

"You mean your cookbook?" I jumped to my feet. "You planted it in the cabin. You knew I would find it there."

"Um, no, I didn't," said Denise.

I stared at her.

"I'm serious. We planted the cobwebs and bats, and the spiders, the skeletons—"

"I did the pumpkins," Sheena and Maeve said together.

"No one brought a cookbook," Denise insisted. "Why would we? It doesn't even look scary. Not unless you open the cover—"

"And watch the slugs pour out, yeah." I scowled at her. "Hilarious prank, by the way. So sweet of you to leave it out on my porch last night."

The girls looked completely confused.

"Slugs? We filled a cookbook with slugs?"

"Wow, Tammy really is crazy."

"No way we did that. No way."

I let out a growl. "You know what? Forget it. I don't believe a word you say anyway. You just lie, lie, lie. Every word coming out of your mouth is a—"

THUMP!

Everyone gasped as Mrs. McAfee banged through the sliding glass door. Her wine glass was gone, replaced in her hand by a plastic container.

My cookie box.

"Ammmmzzzznngg!" she slurred. "Jsssst inccrrredddbble!" She paused to swallow her cookie. "I never thought I'd live to taste these cookies again. I thought they'd vanished forever!"

Mrs. McAfee suddenly turned to me, beaming.

"Chef Clarisse…Clarisse's cookies…you made them! You actually made them!"

22

SILENCE FELL. THE ONLY SOUND was Mrs. McAfee's mouth, munching cookies.

"Moooooommm!" Sheena whined. "Go away. This isn't funny or cool."

Mrs. McAfee looked at me. "Is there anything I can get you, Clarisse? I mean, Tammy? Do you like my bracelets? Here. Have them."

Mrs. McAfee tried to hand me her solid gold bracelet. Sheena, Maeve and Denise let out gasps. So did I. This was too weird for a prank. No one was this good at acting.

My mind raced. I thought back to Pete's strange reaction. Hadn't Pete been just as obsessed with my cookies? The slugs hadn't bothered him, either. A shiver ran through me. There was something very, very odd about these cookies!

I watched as Sheena and Maeve slowly reached for a cookie. Their wrists trembled. I saw the confusion in their knitted-up eyes.

Should I stop them? I wondered.

Too late. They were already eating. I held my breath as they nibbled the cookies' soft outer edge—and then stiffened, as if they'd both been electrified.

"Tammy, oh my God!"

"Tammy made these? Tammy Tammy?"

Denise frowned at them. "Don't be dumb. Let's do something else, okay?"

Sheena and Maeve traded looks.

"Does Tammy want to?"

"Whatever Tammy wants, we should do."

"Ugh! This isn't funny, you guys!"

Denise stalked toward the cookie box. Finding it empty, she shoved me into a wall (even though I wasn't blocking her) then snatched a cookie out of Maeve's open mouth.

Half a cookie.

She raised it to her lips. I didn't even think about stopping her. This was it. My big moment! I snaked an arm behind my back. With my hand hidden, I tapped on Sheena's third laptop.

"Circle Girls...Broadcasting Live!" said the screen, just as Denise's teeth pierced the soft cookie crust.

"This is so awful," she grumbled. "So disgusting. So—oh my God—so DELICIOUS!" Her green eyes almost popped in amazement.

As for me, I knew a priceless opportunity when I saw one. With a wide grin, I turned toward the live-streaming laptop.

"TammyBakes, that's me! Heart and subscribe for more jaw-dropping recipes!"

23

"BYE, TAMMY!"

"Later!"

"See you at school!"

Sheena, Maeve and Denise waved through a gap in the stretch Hummer's sunroof next morning. I grinned back ferociously. I was still climbing my driveway when a voice shouted, "Tammy! Wait!"

It was Sheena, rushing up for a hug.

"Call you later, okay?"

"Um, sure," I said.

Mom and Dad couldn't believe my good mood when I walked in the door.

"Well, well, well! Where was this in the forecast?"

"How was the mansion, kiddo? Did you sleep like a princess and chat with Brad Pitt?"

I started to laugh. Then I screamed as a big, hairy spider legged up to me.

"Aragol, no! Don't eat the princess!" Pete cackled and scooped up his 'pet', a disgusting tarantula.

"Ew, Pete!" I snapped. "Put your spider away!"

"Okay." Pete cupped the tarantula and walked it back to its tank. Mom and Dad stared in amazement.

"Since when is your brother so helpful?" said Mom.

"Teach me," Dad begged.

I thought for a moment. "I have an even better idea."

"UGH, TAMMY, this is totally gross!"

"Keep digging, Denise. Thirty-two slugs. Check the filters again."

Denise sank her perfect fingernails into the muck. I couldn't stop laughing. I'd called Sheena a few minutes earlier, asking for help, and guess what? The stretch Hummer zoomed back! It was presently idling in the street while Denise—just Denise—did her work.

The work I'd requested.

The work she couldn't refuse, because somehow, the Chiller Cookies had placed the Circle Girls under my spell.

I know.

I KNOW.

"Is there anything else?" asked Denise, tossing the last slug in the jar.

"Nope," I said. "That's it." *For now.*

I snickered as Denise zombie-walked back to the Hummer. According to Maeve, she gagged for ten minutes straight.

Sheena sent me the clip. It was great.

On my way inside, I heard Dad and Pete talking.

"How about a catch, Pete? You've got Fall Ball next weekend."

"Can't. I'm hunting cockroaches with Aragol. So far he's only caught the one in your shower."

"C-Cockroaches?" Dad spluttered. "Shower? *Whose* shower?"

I waited until Dad's panicked voice disappeared up the hall. Then I tiptoed into the kitchen. No one noticed the slug jar beneath my left arm.

And okay, I know what you're thinking. I'm a psychic, remember?

Mind control. What is it? How does it work? And seriously, Tammy, why are cookies involved?

The same questions rolled through my head as I mixed the ingredients. I couldn't answer them either.

But did I care? Did I let my ignorance stop me?

No.

As far as I was concerned, the Chiller Cookies *worked.* They made people happy. Gloriously, crazily happy. They made people turn to me, beaming, and say, "Tammy, you genius, you're the greatest chef ever!" or "Tammy, let's shoot a new video together!" or "Tammy, welcome to the Circle Girls, you're officially in charge of our group!"

Did I mention that #TammyBakes was now a trending topic online? I got the news from Sheena last night, after one of our lipsync dance sessions.

Amazing, right?

Okay, so I made one small mistake. I originally thought the cookbook was a prank from Denise—a Halloween cookbook—when actually it was a real cookbook with real gourmet recipes.

Genius recipes.

I had it all figured out. The slugs weren't supposed to be gross. They were just...*unexpected.* A kind of top secret ingredient that most people never thought of adding to cookies.

How cool was that?

As I said before, I *love* mixing weird stuff together. It's the most mystical, magical part about baking. Vinegar on its own is disgusting. Baking flour tastes like dry dirt. But in a recipe, if you combine them correctly...

Voila! Genius food! So why not slugs?

Maybe the mind control is a bonus, I thought. *The side effect of eating true gourmet food.*

Was that why certain chefs got so rich and successful? Was that how they sold all those cookbooks?

Since I still wasn't sure, I decided to test my theory on Mom and Dad. I wanted to see what would happen if they ate Chiller Cookies.

Could I really control them? Could I make them think it was Christmas tonight (for example) and on every night after?

"AH, THERE'S MY warm summer breeze!"

Mom beamed as I laid my finished cookie tray onto the table. Dad closed his laptop and blinked, just as Pete elbowed in, loudly sniffing the air.

"Cookies! *Cookies! COOKIES!*"

"Chill, Pete," I laughed. "There's enough for you, too."

I grinned as I passed the Chiller Cookies around. I had no fear at all. I knew exactly what was going to happen.

So why was my heart speeding up?

"These roasted almonds look strange," said Dad, squinting.

That's because they aren't roasted almonds, I thought.

"No soy sauce, I hope?" Mom asked worriedly.

I laughed. "No, Mom. They're not sour brownies, I swear."

"If you say so." Mom and Dad traded looks. "On the count of three," they said, making a big joke of things. "One—two—"

CRRRRRNNNCH!

Everyone bit down on their cookies. I felt a rush of excitement as they noisily chewed and swallowed, making these weird, dreamy faces.

Which quickly became weird, creeped-out faces.

"Holy tornado," Mom spluttered.

Dad's face turned pea-green. "Poison…poisoned…"

"Unnngghh," said Pete, retching. "I think I'm gonna be—"

"So am I—"

"Uh oh—"

"BLEEECHHHH!"

Mom, Dad and Pete opened their throats, releasing a thick spray of vomit. For a long time, I couldn't stop screaming.

"THIS WAS A CLOSE CALL," Dr. Lubin, the clinic doctor, said seriously. "You all could have died."

"I've never *seen* so much puke," said a nurse.

I bowed my head without speaking. I sat alone in the waiting room, shivering like a rabbit. My mind spun around and around.

How could this happen?

What went wrong with my second batch of Chiller Cookies?

On the way home, we stopped for supplies at the pharmacy. I offered to run inside with the credit card.

"No, I think you've done enough for today, Tammy," Mom answered.

Dinner that night was Perrin's Pizza. Nobody ate. Me, because I couldn't stop thinking of eyeballs. Everyone else, due to crippling, gut-wrenching sickness.

I apologized to Mom, Dad and Pete. I brought them napkins when they needed them, and replaced their used puke bags. I even tried clearing the dinner plates—but Dad stopped me on the edge of the kitchen.

"Need something?" I asked. "Another puke bag?"

Dad's expression was strange. He leaned forward and kissed my ponytail. Then he plunged a knife through my heart, killing me instantly.

"Sorry kiddo," he said. "Your Mom and I spoke. For the rest of the month, we think it's best if you steer clear of the kitchen. You're banned."

24

I FINALLY FELL ASLEEP around midnight. I was so pan-icked. So gloomy. No wonder I ended up where I did.

"Taaaaammmmy," sang a voice. "Taaaaammmmy."

My feet moved without warning. One minute, I was curled up in bed. The next, I was off—out the door, down the creaky wood steps.

Stop, I thought. *Stop. Turn around.*

I felt like a dog on a leash. I could not stop my feet from descending the stairs. At the same time, a strange feeling stirred in my chest. Some part of me wanted to sprint down the steps. To greet the voice that had sum-moned me.

My heart jolted.

Was this how Denise felt?

Was this why the Circle Girls obeyed my commands?

"Taaaaammmmy," the voice repeated. "Taaaaammmmy."

At the end of the staircase, my feet swiveled right, to-ward...*the place.*

Not the kitchen that belonged to my house.

A different place. The Dream Kitchen.

"Hello, Chef Clarisse," I said. "Hello...Grigory."

My voice shook as I spotted the mummy chef, twirling his knife.

Chef Clarisse beckoned me closer. She looked even prettier tonight. Her perfect skin was so silky, I felt a stab of guilt as she twisted it into a frown.

"Tsk, tsk. This will not do at all."

She took my hand and led me across the kitchen. We stopped in front of a towering, six-foot-tall oven.

My heart jolted. Was she going to cram me inside?

No. The oven was cold, thank the Lord. I let out a shivery breath, watching it fog up the oven glass. Slowly the fog disappeared, revealing a crystal-clear image.

Me. My own face.

With an ugly green wart on my forehead!

I almost screamed when I reached up and touched it.

A wart! A real wart!

I turned to Chef Clarisse. "What's going on? What just happened?"

"Take a guess, child. Search your memory. Surely you realize that something went wrong."

My eyes bulged. "M-My second batch of Chiller Cookies? I don't understand! I followed the instructions. I did everything right. But my family got really sick. They almost died."

"Of course they did." Chef Clarisse glared at me. "The Grand Desserts are unique. They can be prepared only one time per person. After that, they will lose their...*effectiveness.*"

"I...I didn't know."

"Ignorance of the rules is no excuse. Naturally, *The Booke of Loste Foodes* is extracting its price."

I cringed as Chef Clarisse tapped my forehead wart.

"Tammy, Tammy, Tammy," she sighed. "I am *so* disappointed in you. I thought you possessed more drive. More ambition. I thought you would complete *The Booke of Loste Foodes* at all costs. Yet here you are, repeating the First Grand Dessert, like a brainless beginner."

Chef Clarisse's scarlet eyes raked across me. I wanted to melt through the floor.

"I-I'm sorry," I stammered. "H-How can I…fix this?"

"Complete the Second Grand Dessert," she said at once.

"But I can't even read it. The text…it's too blurry."

Chef's Clarisse's lip curled in a sneer. "I cannot decide if you are lazy or just foolish. Having completed the First Grand Dessert, you should have noticed the Second Grand Dessert is now visible. When was the last time you opened *The Booke*? Tsk. Tsk. My greatest treasure. Yet you do not even read it!"

My heart trembled. She was right. I hadn't checked *The Booke* since completing the first batch of Chiller Cookies.

"And the wart?" I said shakily.

"Complete the Second Grand Dessert," Chef Clarisse repeated. "This will not only restore your appearance, it will even improve it. For a time. Naturally, you must complete the Third Grand Dessert to maintain your good looks. And the Fourth."

"And the Fifth," I sighed, sensing a pattern. "And the Sixth after that. And the—"

"*No.*" Chef Clarisse cut in sharply. "Four is all I require."

My breath quickened. "And then what? If I bake the Four Grand Desserts, what happens? Will I be brilliant and cute and successful? Can I launch my own cookbooks?"

Chef Clarisse's scarlet eyes flashed.

"If you do this, Tammy—if you fulfill your vow to *The Booke*—you will tap your truest potential. You will fully blossom."

She licked her lips.

"Four pages. Four Grand Desserts. Complete them, and everything you've ever wished for will be instantly and permanently yours. You will embody it all."

AFTER OUR EXCHANGE, Chef Clarisse let me tour the Dream Kitchen. I couldn't believe how well-stocked it was. She showed me all her top-grade appliances, then flung the cabinet doors wide, revealing row upon row of ingredients. She had *everything*. Flour and baking soda. Sugar and vanilla. Even soy sauce!

"Yours," Chef Clarisse said simply. "From now on, Tammy, consider yourself an honored guest of my kitchen. You may visit whenever you like. And not only that—"

Her scarlet eyes flicked to the corner.

"My assistant, Grigory, will help you. Grigory can handle many intricate tasks you cannot. He is quite skilled, I assure you."

My good mood instantly soured. *Grigory? Awful Grigory?*

I looked up and saw the mummy chef twirling his knife. My heart shivered.

"Can you c-control him?" I asked Chef Clarisse.

"Why, of course." Her smile sharpened. "I control everything that enters my kitchen. Everything. This is the power *The Booke* has given me."

I thought for a moment. "About this power...So the Grand Desserts turn people into our fans, right? Like, super fans? They do whatever we ask them to."

"Correct. The Servant Spell is quite strong."

"Huh? Servant Spell? Like a *magic* spell?"

"Magic? No. Of course not." Chef Clarisse tittered. "'Servant Spell' is just a silly name I came up with. This is the art of baking, child. Not witchcraft."

Chef Clarisse laughed again. I felt a strange queasiness in my stomach, especially after Grigory's laughter joined in.

I had so many questions. How long did this fan thing— the Servant Spell—last for? Did it work on anyone? Would other Grand Desserts have even stronger effects?

Finally, Chef Clarisse raised a hand. "Another time, child. The hour grows late. There is a final rule I must impart before leaving you."

"Another rule?"

Chef Clarisse smiled. "For each Grand Dessert that we bake together, you—and only you—must provide the final ingredient. You must collect it yourself. My kitchen can supply many things, child, but never that. Do you understand?"

I thought for a moment, then nodded. It was still a generous offer. With the Dream Kitchen supporting me, I wouldn't need to make up excuses to borrow Mom's credit card. I had all the groceries I needed right here.

Almost.

One ingredient, I thought. *Only one. How hard could it be?*

Feeling a bit better, I waved goodbye to Chef Clarisse. As I turned to go, I heard a low moan. Grigory stepped forward. His single blue eye gleamed like ice through his slithery face wrap.

"Byyyyyyeeeeee," he rasped.

It was the ugliest sound I'd ever heard in my life.

AS SOON AS I got upstairs, I rushed to the bathroom. My eyes stretched as I saw myself in the mirror.

The wart was still there. Green and wiggly.

I almost threw up in the sink. My brain twisted. I was having serious doubts about using the Dream Kitchen. But what choice did I have?

Back in my room, I grabbed *The Booke of Loste Foodes* and flipped to page two. I had a nasty feeling about the Second Grand Dessert.

Guess what else? I was right.

SPIDER HOLE DONUTS
THE SECOND GRAND DESSERT

My eyes slid down the page. I think I already knew what I'd find.

FINAL INGREDIENT ALERT!
SPIDER INNARDS (MASHED, 3OZ. MINIMUM)

My blood chilled. *Spiders. Mashed spiders.*

I glanced in my bedroom mirror. I saw myself trembling and shaking. My green wart looked bigger and grosser than ever. How would I ever get rid of it?

"Spiders," I whispered. "Spider *innards.*"

I let out a moan.

25

"THERE SHE IS!"

"The girl from the videos!"

"She's so famous, she's hiding her face in a hood!"

Whispers followed me up the halls and into my Monday classes. Wherever I went, people pointed and stared. I felt like some kind of mystical being crossing into their presence.

I kind of was, wasn't I?

"Tammy, over here! Sit here!"

The Circle Girls motioned me over. I beamed, walking up to Denise's throne seat.

"Ooh, this looks comfy." I laughed at Denise's shocked face as Sheena and Maeve pinned her arms, dragging her out of the seat.

"Much better," I said, plopping down.

"Is there anything else you need?" Denise mumbled.

I glanced at her. Did she look a bit tense? *Maybe I'm pushing her too far,* I thought. *But then again...*

"I could use a cup of water, Denise."

"Of course," she replied, stalking off.

"From the teacher's lounge!" I called after her.

Denise's only reply was a grunt.

Was I enjoying my newfound celebrity? Did I like being known as Tammy Saris, Queen of the Circle Girls—the girl whose web channel was blowing up on the Internet?

Yes and no.

On one hand, I was now popular enough to start my own accidental fashion trend—wearing a really, really big hood during class. On the other, I was only wearing the hood to cover up the wart on my forehead.

I couldn't let ANYONE see it. How could a celebrity have an ugly green wart? How could she sell zillions of cookbooks, and also be a star on TV, when her face was so ugly, it literally grossed people out?

I have to fix this, I thought crazily. *I have to bake the Spider Hole Donuts and restore my appearance. Which means I have to collect three ounces of...of...*

"Miss Saris, are you paying attention?" Mr. Trevors interrupted.

I blinked and looked up.

"Yes she is!" Maeve announced.

"She definitely is," Sheena added.

"Thank you, peanut gallery," Mr. Trevors sighed. Then the classroom door opened, and Denise spilled my water cup all down her blouse.

Because I told her to.

IN THE HALL AFTER CLASS, my eye flashed on one of the bulletins.

Attention all goblins and ghouls! Strap on your cursed aprons and set your cauldrons to bubble and trouble! It's that time of year again…

THE HALLOWEEN BAKE OFF!
— Fun! Food! Surprises!
— Prizes awarded, all age groups.
— Saturday, October 31st 1-2pm (come early!)

Note: You needn't be a chef to enjoy a FIVE-STAR experience! Come to Field 2C to cheer our contestants, sample spooky new recipes, and learn the shocking truth about our top secret MYSTERY JUDGE!

"I wonder who the mystery judge is?" I said to myself. I almost gasped when a boy's squeaky voice responded.

"Ms. Carlton says the judge is a celebrity chef! Isn't that cool? My friend Alan thinks it's Tammy Saris, from TammyBakes. But I told him it couldn't be her, because— GAAAHHH!"

The boy gave an earsplitting squeak when he saw me. His lips quivered and his cheeks glowed brick-red.

"A celebrity chef?" I repeated. "Are you sure?"

The boy swayed on his feet. He looked starstruck.

So was I—kind of! *A celebrity chef was the judge?* My mind raced. If I fed them one of my special desserts…if I could somehow ensnare them and turn them into my fan…

My *celebrity* fan.

Imagine how fast I could rise with a celebrity talking me up!

My heart fluttered. *Saturday. Next Saturday!*

I knew I couldn't miss it. No way.

EXCEPT FOR STEALING her seat, I left Denise alone during lunch. I was too busy thinking about Spider Hole Donuts.

I knew I still needed spiders. But assuming I found them…Assuming I baked the donuts tonight, Monday night…

Could I get rid of my wart, but save the donuts for Saturday?

Would the donuts stay fresh? Would they…*work*?

The idea was extremely exciting. I didn't want to rely on Chef Clarisse's other recipes. Who knew what kind of freaky ingredients they required?

"Hem hem!" said a voice.

I blinked, looking up. A wall of sixth-graders was boxing me in.

"Tomorrow is Janine's birthday," someone said.

"You know, Janine Colopoulos?"

"You'll bake for her, right? Like a treat or something?"

"Not just for her, but for all of us?"

I stared at them. *A birthday treat? For tomorrow?* Get real. It was the last thing I needed. I racked my brains, trying to find some excuse to get rid of them—but another voice cut across me.

"*Of course* Tammy will bake for you! She would never miss Janelle's birthday. Never ever! Isn't that right, Tammy?"

I swiveled round. Guess whose pathetic green eyes glittered back at me?

"Freeze!" I snapped. "No talking!"

Denise's smirk stiffened. There was a CLUNK! as her fork hit the floor.

Too late. Janine's friends were in uproar.

"She will? Tammy will?"

"Tammybakes! Woo!"

"Tomorrow!"

MY LAST CLASS OF THE day couldn't come soon enough. I had two reasons for bursting into science lab ahead of everyone else. The first was to snag a seat in the back, before anyone else roped me into baking more birthday desserts.

The second was spider-related.

"Um, Mr. Murray?" I asked. "How much does a spider weigh? How many spiders would it take to weigh exactly three ounces?"

My cheeks reddened. I wouldn't have dared to ask anyone else. But Mr. Murray is super laid back. His tests are full of comic strips and goofy word problems, like with werewolves and vampires duking it out.

"Wow, a spider question!" Mr. Murray's eyes lit up. "What a coincidence. Did you steal that question from Friday's pop quiz?"

Several kids groaned at the joke.

"Let's see. Three ounces is approximately eighty-five grams. A common spider weighs less than one gram. A lot less. So to fill three ounces, you would need, hmm— what's the scientific term for it? Oh, right. *Hundreds of spiders!*"

My eyes boggled. "Hundreds?"

Mr. Murray grinned. "If they're tiny, you might need a thousand."

One thousand spiders!

Where would I find them? How would I do it?

"This is all theoretical, of course, Tammy? I hope you aren't planning a second career as Spider-Woman, fighter of crime. If you are, I'm afraid you'll be sorely disappointed. Emphasis on the sore part. Yowza! Some of those bigger spiders can bite!"

I smiled weakly.

"Well, it's your decision!" Mr. Murray turned to the rest of the class. "Onward, to our next topic: dissections! We will be poking and prodding some *interesting* specimens in the coming days. None as cuddly as spiders, I'm afraid— but close, very close. So you must come prepared!"

I didn't like the way Mr. Murray grinned at the freezer in back of the lab. What did he keep in there? What was he planning?

Ugh. I could worry about that later. For now, I needed to focus on spiders. Finding them. Storing them. Sliding my finished Spider Hole Donut tray into the oven…

No. Into *Chef Clarisse's* oven. Deep in the Dream Kitchen.

My heart quivered. Was I crazy? Was it actually, physically possible to bake food in that horrible place?

I touched the wart on my forehead.

Yes, I thought crazily. *The Dream Kitchen is real. I can use it.*

I had to.

26

OUT IN THE PARKING LOT, I watched as Sheena and Maeve blew me kisses from the stretch Hummer's sunroof. The Circle Girls had a poetry project due tomorrow. I thought about making them hunt spiders for me anyway, but in the end, I decided against it. I wasn't that evil.

So I just asked Denise.

"Owwwww! Tammmmy! IT BIT ME!"

I laughed as Denise tossed a tiny black spider into the bag I held out.

One down, I thought. Hundreds to go.

"Should we check the forest trail?" Denise blurted out.

I glanced at her. Were her eyes twinkling? Was that sass I detected?

No. Denise is under my spell. She has to follow my orders.

My eyes drifted across the school grounds, to the towering treetops. I knew we could find spiders if we looked there. The forest trail was crawling with bugs.

But what else was it crawling with?

I hadn't forgotten the one-eyed squirrels, or the cabin at the end of the trail. Jake's cabin.

A shiver ran through me. Was Jake Aberforth a living boy or a ghost? Did he haunt the forest trail, like Denise had once claimed?

I didn't know. I didn't want to know.

"Forget the woods," I told Denise. "I have a better plan, actually."

Ten minutes later, Hoberville's dorkiest biker gang wheeled into view. Its nine members wore striped socks and dusty Pirates baseball uniforms.

My brother Pete was in front, grinning like crazy.

"You're friends with Denise Daddario?" a gang member marveled.

Pete puffed out his chest. "Arr! I'm a pirate!"

"No, you're a second basemen—a shortstop if Ben Schwartz is pitching."

They started to squabble.

"Quiet!" I snapped. "You aren't pirates or shortstops. You're my spider patrol squad. Pete, split your friends into groups. Take control!"

"Arrr!" Pete replied. "I mean, yes."

Within seconds, Pete had the Pirate teams settled. It was amazing how quickly he worked, even without a 'Servant Spell' helping him. Although it didn't hurt that one of the prettiest girls in school walked beside him.

For the next two hours, Pete and his Pirates scoured every cranny and nook of Hoberville Park. They paid special attention to the baseball fields. Both the dugouts and the concession stand yielded several huge specimens.

"Garden spiders," said Pete. "Up to three inches long. Aren't they cute?"

I shivered as a spider scuttled back and forth on Pete's arm.

"Oh sick," said Denise. "Why does your brother love bugs?"

"Because I am one!" Pete cried. "A mosquito!"

Denise screamed as Pete lunged at her, gnashing his teeth. It was pretty hilarious.

But Denise's question got me thinking. Why did Pete know so much about bugs? Because of Aragol. Duh!

How could I forget my little brother had a pet tarantula? And how heavy was Aragol? Three ounces? Four? That spider was huge.

My skin prickled. I was kind of happy I'd forgotten Aragol. The thought of hurting him twisted my stomach. I was okay with catching these little runt spiders, but not Aragol. Not someone's pet.

"We did it! We found the motherlode!"

Four Pirates came sprinting out of the jungle gym, waving my sealed plastic bag like a pirate flag. A completely black pirate flag. I couldn't believe all the spiders they'd crammed into it.

"Babies!" they exclaimed. "Lots of babies!"

Pete scurried over. "Wow, a nest! Is that enough spiders, Tammy? Are you thrilled and impressed?"

Yes and no. I was terrified. Wrists trembling, I pinched the top of the bag, then flung it across the pavement as fast as I could.

"Only one thing to do." I raised my boot in the air. I couldn't wait to stomp all over the spiders. To mash them into goop and guts—into innards, like the recipe said. I mean, seriously. Who wants to handle live spiders?

Looking back, I should have ordered Pete or Denise to do it. But I was too hasty. I wasn't thinking clearly.

"Noooo!" shouted Pete. "Stoooopp! We can't KILL them!"

Pete scooped the bag up and ran. I tried to grab him, to command him to stop, but Pete was too sneaky. He popped the seal on the bag, releasing all the trapped, wriggling spiders.

Yes. He dumped them on top of my head.

"AaaaAAHHhh!" I screamed. "AaaaaaAAAHHHHH! AaaaaaaaaAAAaaaaAAhhhh!"

I thought I would die. Suddenly my hair felt alive, like Medusa. Spiders crawled down my face and into my nose. I screamed and beat them away. But they kept coming. I felt their awful legs poking into my skin. I pictured them creeping into my ears, sinking their poison fangs in my brain and sucking it dry.

How long did I scream for? No idea. I don't remember if I shook the spiders off quickly, or after five awful minutes. All I know is, at some point, the nightmare I was picturing changed. Instead of a billion spiders crawling inside me, suddenly it was only one spider.

A tarantula.

I pictured it crawling out of my nostril and into a mixing bowl.

27

I WOKE UP UNUSUALLY LATE Tuesday morning. I don't know why. Did something happen last night? Was my sleep interrupted?

I rolled out of bed with a yawn. Then I crossed to the mirror.

"Gone," I said. "Vanished."

I ran a finger across my silky-smooth forehead. *No wart.* I raced into the bathroom for a closer look—and to wash the sticky donut glaze off my fingers.

How did *that* get there?

My blood chilled as I remembered my dream last night.

How I walked down my regular staircase. How the Dream Kitchen appeared at the bottom. How Chef Clarisse took my hand, guiding me to the oven, where a huge spider wriggled in Grigory's fist.

"Isss this the onne?" he rasped. *"Thhe finnall ingreddientt?"*

Chef Clarisse nudged me. "Tell him yes, child. A simple nod will suffice. Grigory will handle the rest."

I racked my brains, thinking back to the dream. *Did I nod?*

My thoughts were cut short by a miserable wail.

"MOOMM! DAAADD! WHERE IS ARAGOL?"

Oh no. I pinched the bridge of my nose.

"There's no proof," I whispered. "No one saw you last night. Even if they did, it wasn't your fault. It was Grigory. *Grigory.*"

I counted to ten before I entered the dining room. Mom and Dad stood on top of their seats, peering down at the floor.

"First it was cockroaches," Dad muttered. "Now it's killer tarantulas, roaming the house."

"Aragol isn't a killer!" Pete whined. "He's a lover of meat. And he would never leave his tank. Never ever!"

After a long sweep of the hallway, Dad took his chances and entered the kitchen. "Egg and cheese biscuits," he announced. "Sound good, Pete?"

Pete barely grunted.

"I'll help!" I volunteered. I skipped toward the kitchen—but Mom blocked me off.

"Sorry, Tam. The kitchen is a no-fly zone, remember?"

"Oh. Right." My shoulders slumped.

"You are always welcome in the Dream Kitchen," said an unknown voice in my ear. *"Tell your brother what you did last night. How you grabbed his spider and—"*

"No!" I blurted out. "It wasn't me! I'm not the person who—"

"Tammy, whoa, you're raging like a cyclone!" Mom squeezed my wrists to stop me pounding the air. "Who are you talking to, sweetie?"

My lips quivered. "N-No one, Mom. It's n-nothing, just—"

"YAOOWW! HOT! HOT! HOT!"

A piercing shriek rose from the kitchen. Dad shoved his burnt fingers under the faucet as Mom bustled up to him.

"Honey! Are you all right? What happened?"

"Someone left the stove on. I almost cooked my own hand!" Dad narrowed his eyes at me. "Was it you, Tammy? Were you using the kitchen?"

My face paled. *Oh God. I was, wasn't I? I was down in the kitchen!*

"No," Dad interjected. "Of course not. I've been up for hours. I would have seen you."

I'm not sure you would have, I thought crazily.

"That blasted stove needs replacing," said Mom. "This whole kitchen is falling apart!"

Yes, I thought. *Yes, it is.*

FIVE MINUTES BEFORE the school bus arrived, I was flat on my back, rummaging under my bed. Besides my bookbag, I had one thing to grab.

A secret thing.

THUMP!

My bedroom door opened as Pete thundered in. His red eyes were shriveled from crying, and he was squeezing his fists like he wanted to hit someone.

Me, I realized.

"Did you do it?" Pete demanded. "Did you hurt Aragol? Is that why he's missing?"

Bile rose in my throat. A part of me wanted to explain everything. The wart—*The Booke of Loste Foodes*—the Dream Kitchen that whisked me out of bed every night, making me do things.

Horrible things.

Another part of me quivered with anger. So what if Pete cried? He shouldn't have dumped SPIDERS on my head! He was my servant! He should've *never* betrayed me!

A wild rage burned inside me. Suddenly my brain filled with vile ideas. Twisted thoughts. I wanted to punish Pete even more. I wanted to shove his head in a freezer and—

Whoa. I stopped myself from lunging at Pete. I forced myself to relax. To stop thinking such horrible things. What was wrong with me? What was happening inside of my head?

I turned to Pete. As hard as I tried, I couldn't keep the rage from my voice. "I thought spiders should be set free," I spat. "Isn't that what you told me? Isn't it what Aragol would've wanted?"

Pete's eyes stretched. "Y-You wouldn't!" His lips parted. Any second, he was going to scream. To yell for Mom and Dad. To rat me out! *My own servant!*

"S-Stop!" I commanded. "F-F-Freeze!"

I watched as Pete's lips slammed together. His feet turned to stone. When I felt sure the spell wouldn't break, I crawled under my bed and retrieved a sealed plastic bag.

My Spider Hole Donuts.

I stuffed them into my bookbag, then looked back at Pete. Anger swelled in his eyes. He knew the donuts were fresh. He knew I'd obviously baked them last night.

"Don't tell Mom and Dad," I said. "That's an order."

Pete let out a moan. He didn't want to follow the order. He wanted to break free of the spell and escape. But how could he?

An evil grin touched my lips.

Except something was happening. Something was wrong.

Pete's feet started shaking. His arms wobbled. Then his fingers. His lips.

"ARGGGGHHHHH!" Pete cried out.

There was a loud CRACK! as the Servant Spell shattered.

Pete was free.

And he raced out the door.

28

"MOOMM! TAMMY BROKE THE RULES. SHE'S
BEEN—GRRGGHGGH!"

Pete's screaming cut off as I lunged at him. Gripping
his shirt sleeves, I crazily whipped him around, then did
the only thing I could think of.

I crammed a Spider Hole Donut down his throat.

He was still choking when Mom and Dad rushed upstairs.

"Pete, sweetie? What's wrong?"

"Did you, er, find the spider?"

Pete raised a shivering finger. At me.

"I-It's Tammy!" he gasped "She's—she's"—I held my
breath as Pete swallowed the donut—"a WONDERFUL
chef. That's all. I'm sorry I screamed."

I SPENT THE ENTIRE bus ride checking my face in the
window. My fingers rubbed the spot where my wart disappeared. I still couldn't believe it.

Maybe it's just coincidence, I thought. What if stress caused the wart, and my happiness made it vanish completely?

My thoughts turned to Pete. I pictured his pale, lifeless eyes as he waved goodbye to me. I felt suddenly sick.

I'm sorry, Pete. I'm sorry for hurting Aralog. But I didn't have a choice. I had to follow the recipe. I had to trust Chef Clarisse.

A loud voice interrupted my thoughts.

"Hey! You're Tammy Saris, right? TammyBakes from the Internet? OMG. You're, like, totally famous!"

Joy flooded into me. All my fears sank away as I looked up at a jittery girl in blonde pigtails. My fan.

"Yeah," I smiled back. "I guess I kind of am famous. Aren't I?"

APPARENTLY JANINE COLOPOULOS and her friends were all blabbermouths, because an even bigger wall of kids was waiting for me inside of my first period math class.

"I must be losing my mind," Mr. Trevors said, wiping his glasses. "Seventeen I expected. But thirty-eight? And two more, behind the hydrangea plant! Forty pupils. Good God. Is my course on algebraic expressions this popular? Has my dearest dream come to life?"

There was a pause as every head in the room turned to me.

"I think not," Mr. Trevors said stiffly. "Miss Saris, would you care to enlighten me on this strange situation?"

I smiled and fluffed out my hair. "Would you like a donut hole, Mr. Trevors?" I reached into my bookbag and drew out a silvery orb. The sticky donut glaze shone in the light.

"Ohhhhhh!" moaned the class.

Mr. Trevors seized his ruler, pointing it like a spear, for protection, as a crazed-looking student ran up.

It was Janine Colopoulos.

"Stay back!" Sheena and Maeve warned. They leapt to their feet, forming a rope with their arms. Janine cannonballed into it! Things got so nuts, even Denise came to help. Her green eyes twinkled as she rushed to my seat— my throne seat—and gave it a nasty hip-check.

"Oops," gasped Denise.

My bookbag flew out of my arms. For a split second, it seemed to freeze in mid-air. Then it smushed to the ground, spilling Spider Hole Donuts in every direction.

It was pandemonium! Janine and her friends mobbed the floor, like crazed janitors. I was horrified. The whole time, all I could think about was something Chef Clarisse had told me last night.

"The Spider Hole Donuts look small, but they pack a powerful punch. They are also quite plentiful. Use them wisely, and your fame will spread like wildfire."

She wasn't wrong. By mid-afternoon, there was a new queen of Hoberville Middle School.

Me.

29

"GOING ONCE, GOING TWICE—"

"Wait! Don't stop the bidding! Five! Five fruit roll-ups!"

"Five HOMEWORK assignments! Please, just gimme the donut!"

Technically, I'd been semi-famous for a couple of days now—ever since #TruthOrScare—but Tuesday's lunch was my first taste of real-life celebrity.

Everyone was talking about my Spider Hole Donuts. They found excuses to come up to me. The nervous ones giggled and tugged my clothes. Others stared at my face. One girl started combing my hair while I ate.

So really, it wasn't a shock when the auction began. The boy with an extra Spider Hole Donut, Alex Navarro, opened the bidding at one dollar. His giant feet were planted on top of the lunch table, and he was still taking bids when Vice Principal McKissock stormed into the cafeteria.

"Break it up! Break it up!"

Ms. McKissock sent Alex to detention and confiscated the Spider Hole Donut. The way she squinted down at it reminded me of the movie *Snow White*, with the evil queen clutching the apple.

"This sugar glaze is highly unusual," she murmured. "The tiny fibers are almost *moving*, almost forming a—S-S-Spider!" she shrieked. "I-It's infested! WHO DID THIS?"

Everyone looked at me.

"The glaze does resemble a spider's web," I explained. "But it isn't one. It's sugar. Why don't you taste it and see, Ms. McKissock?"

"I most certainly will not!" she barked. "It's malicious! It's contraband! On your feet, Tammy Saris. You're coming with me."

Ms. McKissock swept forward. The entire cafeteria sprang up to greet her. I saw balled fists and pens held like weapons. Half the kids at the lunch tables gritted their teeth. There were loud hisses—then cheers as Ms. McKissock gave up and retreated.

I slumped in relief. "That's just how fans are," I tried telling myself. "They protect their celebrities. It's normal. Totally normal."

As I sat down again, something squished. I checked my pants pocket.

A donut.

It was the one I'd offered to Mr. Trevors during math class. After my bookbag split open, I'd hunkered down and shoved it into my pocket.

"The last Spider Hole Donut," I whispered.

My eyes flashed. I knew exactly who to give it to.

"DENISE!" I CALLED OUT. "Hey, Denise!"

When she didn't stop, I grabbed her bookbag and dragged her out of Mr. Murray's science lab, where she was trying to hide.

"Don't run away!" Mr. Murray teased. "I've got chilled toads and cow eyes. Come back!"

I laughed at the thought of Denise choosing to dissect a toad rather than talk to me. But I wasn't surprised. I knew my hold on Denise was slipping. She was almost free. I could tell by her actions. But I couldn't just let her escape, could I?

I shoved the donut hole into her palm.

"Eat," I commanded.

"Um, no thanks," said Denise. "I have stomach flu."

"*Eat!*"

I grabbed Denise's palm, pressing it to her lips. She coughed and spluttered. I didn't let go until the entire donut hole was crammed in her mouth.

Then I stood back and watched. I didn't trust Denise for a second. I wanted absolute proof that she swallowed the—

"Ah, there you are!" barked a voice. "Tammy? Tammy Saris?"

I whipped around. Guess who came scurrying up to me?

"Vice Principal McKissock!" I gasped.

My heart raced. I knew I was doomed. But then—

"Oh, I'm so glad I found you, Tammy. So glad! I just wanted to apologize. As for your donut hole…Wow. Just wow!"

Ms. McKissock shook my hand. I caught a whiff of spidery breath as she leaned forward, pressing a note into my palm.

"A list of judges for the Halloween Bake Off," she whispered. "I'm one, so naturally you can count on my vote. As for the others…let's just say, I think they'd appreciate a taste. A little sneak preview. If you know what I mean."

I frowned. *This again?*

"I'm sorry, Ms. McKissock, but if you're asking me to bake *another* dessert, before the Bake Off begins—"

"Oh no. Heavens, no!" Ms. McKissock pretended to gasp. "I just thought, if you happened to bake a bit extra…Even among us teachers, Tammy, your reputation as a chef is considerable. You do want to please your teachers, don't you? You can enter the exact same dessert in the Halloween Bake Off. We don't mind! We just want to sample it early."

I rolled my eyes. How scheming was Ms. McKissock? It was actually scary. No wonder the whole school was afraid of her.

Then I thought some more. Maybe it wasn't such a crazy idea. Wouldn't school be much easier if I turned my teachers into TammyBakes super fans?

"Deal," I replied.

"Excellent!" Ms. McKissock shook my hand again. As she turned to go, I remembered the list she had given me.

"Hey," I said. "Which of these names is the Mystery Judge?"

Ms. McKissock sighed. "The Mystery Judge isn't part of my list. I tried, Tammy. No one knows who it is."

Her heels clicked up the hall, out of sight. I released a sigh into the empty hallway. Then, with a jolt, I remembered Denise.

I spun around. A pair of emerald-green eyes twinkled back at me.

"All finished!" said Denise. "Mmm. So good!"

I stared at her. Had she really eaten the donut? I ran some quick tests, just to make sure.

"Denise, scratch my back."

"Denise, honk like a duck."

"Denise, put your fancy new shoes in the water fountain."

What can I say? She passed the tests with flying colors—and sopping wet knee socks. But I still felt uneasy. I cursed myself for not watching her swallow the donut.

Too bad, I thought. *Maybe next time.*

I had more than a week until the Halloween Bake Off. More than a week to master Chef Clarisse's third recipe and introduce it to Vice Principal McKissock and the rest of the judges.

I grinned to myself. I thought it was plenty of time.

But I had no idea what was coming.

30

TO BE FAIR, I WASN'T totally clueless. I knew the Third Grand Dessert would be difficult. Horrifying, even—at least when it came to the final ingredient.

Who could forget wild slugs? Spider innards?

Whatever it is, I thought, I can do it. I'll manage.

Then I flipped to page three of the cookbook.

BLOOD CAKE
THE THIRD GRAND DESSERT

And the small box of text at the end.

FINAL INGREDIENT ALERT!
BLOOD (HUMAN, 2 TSP.)

"Blood!" I cried out. "Human blood?!"

Acid rose in my throat. I felt ill. Horribly, violently ill.

Where was I going to find blood? And if I didn't find it…If I let that horrible wart reappear…

"Don't freak out," I told myself. "Breathe, Tammy. Breathe. How much blood even is it? A drop? Just a few measly drops?"

I decided to run a quick test. My heart thumped as I tiptoed downstairs, toward the kitchen. I was almost inside when Mom caught me.

"Tammy, whoa—not so fast!" Her eyes scrunched through her crazy winged glasses. "Be honest. Were you trying to sneak into the kitchen?"

Oh man. "I wasn't going to cook, Mom, I swear! I just need to borrow something. A teaspoon."

"A teaspoon of what?"

Blood, I thought crazily.

"Nothing," I said out loud. "Just an empty teaspoon. Well, two."

Mom scrunched her eyes even more. She let me pass with a warning.

"Why do I sense storms in the forecast?" she muttered.

TEN MINUTES LATER, I held the first teaspoon over the sink. My arm quivered. Thank God the downstairs bathroom is locked, I thought. I didn't want anyone to see my next move.

No, I wasn't going to hurt myself. Are you crazy?

With my free hand, I lifted the bottle of cough syrup that Mom kept in her drawer. The syrup was cherry-red, like Denise's cell phone. Like blood.

PLOP!

The first bloody drop hit the teaspoon. The liquid splatted and sloshed, like the blood rushing into my heart. How many drops filled a teaspoon? I wondered.

That was the test. It was information I desperately needed to know before I even considered collecting real blood.

One drop? I could handle it.

Two to three drops? We'll see.

But anything bigger than that…

My heart trembled as more syrup drops splatted the teaspoon.

One, two, three. Four, five, six. SEVEN. EIGHT. NINE.

Nine drops of blood.

And that's just one teaspoon, I thought. Just half what I need.

I let out a gasp. Two teaspoons was a lot of blood.

Where was I going to get it? Who would help me?

As soon as I thought it, a shiver ran through me. I had an idea, all right. A different way to get blood.

My skin prickled as I cleaned the teaspoons and put the syrup bottle back in Mom's drawer. Then I slipped away. Out the door. Up the creaky wood steps.

To find Pete.

31

"YOUR ARM, PETE," I said shakily. "H-Hold it out for me."

"Okay." Pete smiled and followed the order.

We were upstairs in my bathroom. Pete's left arm lay flat across the countertop, like a plank of wood—like a baseball bat—while his right hand gripped a slim ballpoint pen.

I'd already explained the situation to Pete. He'd smiled the same robot smile. He would've agreed to do anything.

I watched with slitted eyes as the pen slowly sank toward his bicep. The soft skin rippled and pulsed.

So did I. My whole body rippled and pulsed.

Could I do it? Could I ask Pete to...? Could I actually...?

No. Yes. I don't know!

I shuddered as the nib of Pete's pen pricked the muscle. I watched the soft skin release, forming a dent where the nib pushed it in. Pete was gritting his teeth. I could sense how afraid he was. Any second, the soft skin would pop. The nib would slide in, like a needle.

And then what? How much blood would come out?

Two teaspoons? More?

I pictured blood spurting out like a geyser. Blood sloshing into the sink. Blood on the walls, on our clothes, as Pete sagged to the floor.

"You killed me, Tammy. I was your number one fan. Now I'm dead."

I opened my eyes. Pete's skin was about to pop. Any second now—

"S-Stoppp!" I cried out. "Don't do it. I changed my mind!"

"Okay." Pete pulled his arm away. "Here's your pen, Tammy." He passed me the slim, uncapped pen with its needle-like nib.

My wrist was shaking so badly, I dropped it.

"I CAN'T DO IT," I moaned. "It's impossible."

I was down in the Dream Kitchen, cringing at Chef Clarisse's cold expression. Grigory stood silent in the corner. His butcher's knife gleamed as he twirled it.

"You swore," Chef Clarisse reminded me. "You took a sacred vow."

"I-I did," I admitted. "But this…it's not normal cooking or baking. Blood? Human blood? You can't feed people blood! It's…it's wrong!"

"This is what The Booke demands of you. This is its price."

"N-No," I stammered. "I-It's too much. Stop. I have to stop."

My throat burned. I was terrified. Shaking all over.

"Stop?" Chef Clarisse's scarlet eyes flashed. "You swore a vow, Tammy. You shared my ingredients. Accepted my generous help. You are, in fact, standing in my kitchen right now." Her lip twisted. "No, child. You may not simply...STOP."

The word struck like a lightning bolt. Even my bones stiffened as I instantly lost control of my body. My lungs emptied. My heart temporarily quit pumping blood. A second later, I felt my consciousness slipping away...

"MmrhRghghhhh!" I cried desperately.

"Foolish. So foolish." Chef Clarisse flicked a finger, releasing me. "Have you not ruthlessly snatched dozens of servants already? Why not request the blood as an offering? You have this power. Why not use it?"

I felt her scarlet eyes boring into me. Reading my thoughts.

"I see. So you were perfectly willing to use the Servant Spell, back when it suited you. And yet, now, you refuse to extract a teensy portion of blood when your master requests it. Tsk tsk. This displeases me. However, you are not the only chef who possesses such power..."

Chef Clarisse's smile contorted. Her scarlet eyes flared in the oven glass, sending chills down my neck. I could not move a muscle.

"Your arm," she said curtly.

My arm jerked in response.

"Grigory. Come."

I heard laughter—hideous, throat-scraping laughter—as Grigory stalked forward. A tall object gleamed in his fist.

Not a pen. A butcher's knife.

I wanted to curl up and scream. But how could I? Unable to move, I just watched, like a spectator, as Chef Clarisse plucked the knife out of Grigory's hand. She pressed the cold handle into my palm.

"Squeeze the knife, Tammy," she commanded. "Now raise it for me. Higher. Higher. Good. Now...sink it into your arm. Can you feel it? Do you see the point sticking in?"

Oh God.

I felt it. The cold knife eating into my flesh. I tried dropping it. I did everything to resist it. But I was powerless against the Servant Spell!

Seconds passed. The knife tip sank lower and lower.

I was going to cut myself open!

32

COLD LAUGHTER RANG IN my ears as Grigory's knife hit the floor with a sickening thud, barely missing my feet.

"Oh thank God," I said, gasping. I felt the Servant Spell crack and release.

"See, Tammy?" Chef Clarisse whispered. "See how easy it is to control our servants? To make them…*do things?*"

"Y-You almost m-made me c-cut m-my arm open!" I spluttered.

"Careful, child. I still might." Chef Clarisse pursed her lips, thinking. "Twenty-four hours," she said suddenly. "I will grant you one last extension. One chance to use the powers I've given you. To fulfill your vow to *The Booke.* To find blood."

My face trembled. "T-Twenty-four hours?"

Chef Clarisse leaned her perfect face closer, grinning wolfishly.

"My patience is not unlimited, child," she whispered. "Nor do I tolerate *weakness.* Did you think a single green wart was unpleasant? Oh dear. I can do far worse than warts, foolish one. *I will have the blood.* One way or another, I'll have it."

Dark laughter filled the silence that followed.

I WOKE UP WITH chills down my spine. *Twenty-four hours.*

Shadows danced on the wall, like black knives, as I crawled out of bed. Chef Clarisse's last words were still haunting me.

I will have the blood. One way or another, I'll—

CLUNK!

My thoughts scattered as something *huge* hit my window. I looked up. The orange curtains were leaping and swaying as the blinds underneath scraped the air.

Open. The window was open.

Someone is out there, I realized. My heart pounded. I slowly stepped toward the window. Slid the curtains apart. Raised my shivering hand to the blinds.

Eyes. A pair of wide, spying eyes. Staring back at me!

Denise? Was it Denise?

No. A boy.

"Whoooaaaa!" he cried out. The ladder underneath him tipped backward. There was a slow creak, then a THUMP! as he crashed to the lawn. I looked out the window in shock.

Dead! He's dead!

My eyes stretched. Horror chewed through my bones as I saw the boy's lifeless body. He looked so tiny, so squashed, that I almost screamed when he hopped to his feet, rejoining a large group of kids on the sidewalk. They caught sight of me staring and whooped.

"It's her! It's her!"

"TAMMYBAKES!"

I slammed the window in anger.

"UH OH! I'M NOT seeing signs of a rainbow!"

Sweat dripped off Mom's face as she skipped through the front door, toward the dining room table.

"The Limber Ladies got an early start this morning," she announced. "We tore up the streets. Three tiny tornados!" She paused, wiping fog off her glasses. "There was a lot of foot traffic, actually—especially in front of our house. Would you know anything about that, sweetie?"

"Mom, lay off me, okay?" I mumbled.

Mom squinted at me. I tried to wriggle away, but there was no hiding it—Chef Clarisse's parting gift to my forehead.

"A wart," I moaned. "Another wart."

"It's a pimple, sweetie. Just acne."

Yeah, sure, I thought. *So how come it's green?*

"By the way," said Mom, still eyeing me, "I found cough syrup stains in the sink. You aren't catching cold, Tammy, are you?"

Oops. "I meant to scrub those away."

"Scrub 'em, then kill 'em with fire." Dad yawned in front of his laptop. "Cough syrup makes you sleepy. No thank you. I've been up all night, trying to finish this project. Five hundred lines of code to review. Buggy code. I'm telling you, the people this company hires…"

"Ahem," said Mom.

"Except for you, hon. You're great." Dad's eyes twinkled beneath his beard stubble. He yawned again. "And since you're so great, love of my life, boss of my boss—or is it my boss's boss?—would you mind refilling my coffee mug? It's the only thing keeping me awake."

Mom laughed. Steam fogged her glasses as she topped off Dad's mug. I finished my cereal bowl, then glanced at Dad with a sneaking expression.

It's the only thing keeping me awake.

My eyes flicked to the main coffee pot on the kitchen counter. I felt a jolt of excitement.

If I drink coffee, I won't fall asleep. Then the Dream Kitchen won't reappear. I'll never have to see Chef Clarisse!

I jumped to my feet. "I'll do the dishes!"

Mom and Dad traded looks. I think Mom was about to say no, until she noticed all of Dad's empty coffee mugs.

"No cooking," she reminded me.

"Okay!"

As soon as I was out of view, I dropped the dishes in the sink, grabbed the coffee pot, and pressed it to my lips. I knew I had to be quick. Mom and Dad could walk in any second.

Slowly, I tipped the coffee pot forward. It was cold, thankfully. Not hot. I pursed my lips, ready to slug down the coffee.

Just do it, I thought. *The faster, the better.*

Bad idea. Very bad.

"Brlrrhgghghghghgh!" I cried out, as cold coffee rushed down my throat. I started choking at once. The taste was so gross! So disgusting! It slopped in my mouth and tried to chew apart my esophagus.

Ugh! I'd rather drink spiders and slugs! I thought crazily.

I was leaning over the sink, vomiting black—solid black—when Mom found me. She let out a wail.

"Storms, girl! I knew it! You're ill!"

33

I DID NOT GO TO school that day. Mom drove me straight to Dr. Lubin. He ran a few basic tests, then summoned Mom and me into his office.

"Tammy's vitals look fine," Dr. Lubin pronounced. "Though I'd still like a sample of blood, just in case."

He led me into the nurses' room. It looked a lot like a kitchen. A kitchen for *blood*. My eyes bulged as I saw all the bags hanging up. I was so distracted, so full of wild ideas, I missed the nurse sneaking up on me.

"Surprise!" she said.

I felt the sharp jab of a needle. I looked left and saw blood seeping out of my arm, through a thin plastic tube. My inner house mouse screamed out.

Blood! BLOOD! BLOOOOODDDD!

My view of the world started flashing.

"She's gonna faint!" barked the nurse. A second nurse gripped my shoulders, barely propping me up.

How ironic, I remember thinking. *I gave my blood to the nurse. If only it was Chef Clarisse who I gave it to…*

Dr. Lubin's voice drifted into my ears.

"Looks like a classic case of food poisoning, Mrs. Saris. Has Tammy been baking again? Mmm. I would keep her far, far away from the kitchen tonight."

*That's…the…idea…*I thought loopily.

Then I really did faint.

CHEF CLARISSE DID NOT reappear in a dream, thank the Lord. I woke up in the car. I shuddered as I realized what a close call I'd just had. What if my fainting had triggered the Dream Kitchen? What if I opened my eyes and saw Grigory's knife?

I spent the rest of the drive shaking in fear. You could say I was pretty high-strung. Mom certainly did.

"Sweetie? Please stop fidgeting."

"You need to relax, Tammy."

"Leave your bandage alone, dear. The wound underneath is still fresh."

The wound underneath.

Five minutes later, I was leaping out of a moving vehicle. Mom couldn't stop me. She was still parking the car as I raced up the driveway and into the house.

Within seconds, I'd locked myself into the bathroom. I wanted absolute privacy while I peeled my bandage away, pinching the soft skin that surrounded my needle wound.

Hard. Harder!

"Ugh." Nothing happened! No blood. Not enough of it, anyway.

Don't look at me like that. Do you think I *wanted* to collect blood for Chef Clarisse? No. And I definitely didn't want to bake with it. But what choice did I have?

I'd sprouted one wart already. What came next? A fishhook nose? Moldy skin blotches? Or what about Grigory, swinging his knife?

The consequences were too sick to imagine. One way or another, I knew I had to find blood. *I had to.*

But how? How would I do it?

Until I figured that out, my plan was the same: Stay awake.

Don't lie down. Don't close your eyes. Never, ever relax.

Constant vigilance!

BY FOUR O'CLOCK in the afternoon, I was ready to plop. By six o'clock, I technically did. My brain conked out. I collapsed across the couch as my eyelids fluttered heavily. Dangerously.

At the last second, my phone beeped. The ringing noise jerked me awake.

"Good idea...setting alarms...every hour..." I told myself.

I let out a long, sleepy breath as I rolled to my feet.

Energy. I needed more energy! But how? Where would I get it?

I wished I could eat or drink something. Not coffee. Soda maybe? Or chocolate? All kinds of foods can keep you awake. Unfortunately, I still felt too queasy. That cold coffee murdered my stomach.

Finally, as a last resort, I did something drastic. Something I'd never, ever normally do. My bedroom floor quaked, with a noise just like migrating elephants.

"Tammy!" Mom called up the stairs. "Are you...*exercising?*"

"Better," I gasped. "Feeling...better..."

My chest heaved and my undershirt dribbled with sweat. Mom climbed the stairs with pursed lips.

"You need to stop, Tammy. You're ill. You should be sleeping!"

"No!" I blurted out. "Just a little longer. Please."

"It's nearly eight o'clock, sweetie—"

"HON!" came Dad's voice, interrupting. "This—software—is—USELESS! Who wrote our compiler, an orangutan? I—I can't fix this! I honestly can't. You have to help me!"

Mom rolled her eyes. "Every deadline he does this. Like clockwork."

I heaved a sigh as she turned down the stairs. Safe. I was safe.

For now. I felt my eyelids flutter. I started jogging again.

How long did I jog for? Hours and hours. I jogged until the night sky filled the windows. Mom and Dad were still working downstairs, on their laptops, and Pete was probably on Xbox. He roared every couple of minutes. But even his roars were growing quieter now.

I glanced at the wall. Twelve o'clock. Midnight.

Was it midnight already?

I suddenly noticed my stomach rumbles felt smoother than before. Less chewed-apart from the coffee.

I can eat now, I realized.

"Oh thank God." My vision blurred as I turned down the stairs. I was dizzy with hunger. *Not for long,* I thought excitedly. *A fizzy drink. A big bowl of grapes. Vanilla yogurt with sugar and—*

"Whoa."

Halfway down the stairs, I gripped the railing in shock. Fear spiked in my throat. Wherever I looked, my vision kept blurring and changing. I pinched my arm, then rubbed my fists on my eyes.

Was I still awake? Was I dreaming?

I felt so delirious. So exhausted. I suddenly realized I had no idea whether I'd gone downstairs in real life, or as part of a dream I'd just entered.

Oh God.

Should I turn back? Should I risk going forward?

"Taaaaammmmy," called a voice. "Taaaaammmmy."

I spun around in alarm, my legs pushing upward.

Back, I thought crazily. *Back up the stairs!*

My bones felt like Jello. I pushed anyway. I knew I had to resist the summoning. I couldn't let myself be sucked down the steps.

"Tammy!" said a different voice. *"Tammy!"*

I looked up at the railing. Someone was reaching out to me. Grabbing my hand. Dragging me up, off the staircase.

Saving my life.

Pete? Was it Pete?

I blinked my eyes, staring at the boy who was still squeezing my hand. I saw his crisp, light-blue eyes. His endlessly wavy brown hair.

I felt my lips sputter. Never in a million years did I think...did I dare to imagine...

"Jake? Jake Aberforth?!"

34

AN EERIE GLOW ROSE FROM the hand Jake extended. He looked ice-cold and slightly transparent.

My eyes widened. "G-Ghost! You're a g-ghost!"

Jake gave a slow smile. "A spirit," he nodded. "I'm sorry for misleading you. My existence is tied to *The Booke of Loste Foodes*. Ever since you started the recipes, I've been trying to reach you. To warn you. Unfortunately, my power is…limited."

WHOOOSH!

I felt an icy chill as Jake's one solid arm disappeared. My hand sank through his fingers, like they didn't exist.

"Jake!" I gasped.

"It's all right. Don't worry about me." Jake swallowed. "You need to listen, Tammy. Mother—Chef Clarisse—she's not who you think she is. She's evil. She has to be stopped."

Jake took a deep breath.

"I'm her servant," he went on. "She enslaved me. It was the first thing she did. I never wanted to give you *The Booke of Loste Foodes*. Mother made me. She put the words in my mouth. She forced me to trick you."

Jake's light-blue eyes glittered.

"But things are different now. I have more power. Mother doesn't realize my strength yet."

"I thought you said your power was limited?"

"With you, yes. Not with Mother." Jake looked at me. "In this world, all that matters is power. I want to use my power to help you, Tammy. I want to erase the vow that you made. If we work together, I can make Clarisse's Kitchen disappear. Forever."

Forever. The word echoed inside of my head.

But was there something odd about Jake's speech? Something familiar?

The thought came and went in a flash, replaced by a flood of relief.

Jake has power! He has a plan to fix everything!

My breath quickened. "Can you…get rid of the Dream Kitchen?"

Jake nodded. "Yes. There is a catch, however. I'm really sorry, Tammy, but there is no way around it. *The Booke of Loste Foodes* has already shown you its Third Grand Dessert. It will not let go of you so easily. If you want to escape, you must gather the final ingredient."

"Blood," I said numbly.

"Yes. *The Booke* is dangerous, Tammy. It has strange and terrible powers. You must collect the blood. Once you have it, do not give it to Mother! Keep it secret. Keep it safe."

"Lord of the Rings," I whispered.

Jake smiled. "A Tolkien fan. Yet another reason I like you." My face turned redder than blood. "Leave the rest to me," he added. "I'll get you out of this, Tammy. I promise."

I found myself believing him. Trusting him.

"Okay," I said quietly.

THUMP! THUMP!

Loud footsteps rose from the staircase.

Jake's ghostly grin faded. "N-No! Mother's found us. He's coming!"

"He?" I cried. *"HE?"*

Ice water flooded my bones. Jake desperately flung out a hand, but I couldn't squeeze it. His entire arm sank through my fingers. I watched his wavy brown hair disappearing.

"Get the blood," Jake said urgently. "Remember…the blood."

He was gone. Vanished. I was still staring, slack-jawed, when a pair of mummy-wrapped hands seized my wrist.

"It'ssss tiiiimmme," rasped a voice.

I gave a strangled yell as Grigory pulled me onto the staircase.

Dragging me down.

Down. Down. Down.

35

BLOODY LIGHT STABBED my eyes as I peeled myself up off the floor, where Grigory tossed me. Chef Clarisse's eyes shone so bright, they lit the room from above.

"I won't…I won't give you blood," I said weakly.

"I suppose not," Chef Clarisse tittered. "Precisely why we must take it. Grigory! Fetch the butcher's knife!"

"Yssss!" Grigory rasped. *"I will extraccct the blood frrr you. I will finnnish ittt!"*

"Noooooo!" I moaned. My heart pounded like crazy. I scrambled onto my feet, dodging Grigory's arms as he lunged at me. I dashed for the staircase. Then, just as Grigory moved to block me, I swerved—

THUMP!

I drove my hips into Chef Clarisse's tiny body. She let out a wail, crunching to the floor like a sack of potato chips.

Whoa, I thought crazily. Also: *YESSS!*

I knew Chef Clarisse could control me. Using the Dream Kitchen had turned me into her servant. So how could I let a single command pass her lips?

Grigory let out a roar. He was still blocking the exit.

"Wwe haave food to baaake, you and I," he rasped.

"Not anymore," I snapped. "Not without blood."

"Therrre wwiill be bloood. Ssoooon. SSOOON!"

With a wild cry, Grigory raised his knife and charged forward, a blur of metal and mummy.

My eyes stretched. The butcher's knife gleamed.

This was it. *Life or death, Tammy.*

I don't know where I found the courage. Was I always this crazy? Because in that moment, with Grigory's knife whipping down, I shot forward. Instead of escaping, I crazily rolled, like a wrecking ball. I pictured myself sliding through the gap between Grigory's legs, like a ninja.

What actually happened was, I *clobbered* his kneecaps.

"AaaaRRRGGGHHHFFFF!!!"

Grigory let out a wail, twisting sideways. Incredibly, he didn't fall over. He was too sturdy.

I didn't care. I sprang to my feet and hit the stairs at a run. I hopped them three at a time.

Clunk. Clunk. Clunk.

My heart was thudding like crazy. I couldn't believe I'd survived. Was that really me back there? Had I just escaped the Dream Kitchen by the skin of my teeth? With a sneak attack?

At the top of the stairs, I caught a last whiff of sugary sweetness.

So long, I thought, as I raced up the hall, toward my bedroom.

My bedroom! *My…bedroom?*

I looked around in a daze. "What the—?"

When did these solid glass shelves get installed? And these pumpkins?

No, I thought crazily. *No. No. NO. NO. NOOOO!*

36

MY EYES ALMOST POPPED and fell out.

Not my house. Not my house. Not my house.

I started crazily rushing around. Past the moldy wood walls. Past the pumpkins that smashed off the—

"Whoaaa!"

My heel hit a wet spot and slid, sending creaks through the floor. Bones clinked together as evil laughter rose from a skeleton. I sank to one knee, feeling numb.

The cabin. I was back at the cabin!

But how? How could this happen?

The Booke is dangerous, Tammy. It has strange and terrible powers.

Is this what Jake meant? Total craziness? *Teleportation?*

Footsteps pounded the stairs as I crawled to my feet. I heard fresh laughter—thicker and rougher than the skeleton's wail.

Grigory.

My blood turned to ice. I slipped again as I tried to speed up. The heavy footsteps drew closer.

"Taaaammmmy," rasped the voice. *"Taaaammmmy."*

Not a sugary voice. Not a voice that I wanted to meet!

Still struggling, still crazily skidding on pumpkins, I opened my throat and said the only words I could think of.

"Jake, help me! Please! Help!"

No response.

I surged ahead, frantically clawing through cobwebs. My lungs heaved and my knees burned with pain. Slow. I was too slow!

Behind me, I heard Grigory's ragged breath. He was gaining ground. Racing me to the rotted front door.

"Jake!" I cried again. "Jake! Are you there?"

"He will not come," Grigory rasped.

I caught a blast of rotten-egg breath as an icy hand grabbed my shirt. I jerked backward, tumbling onto the floor.

Losing the fight.

Grigory towered over me. His single eye blazed through his face wrap. He looked like the celebrity chef of Death's Diner, tagline: Your Last Meal on Earth.

Or wherever this is, I thought crazily.

"Foolish girl," Grigory rasped. *"Jake iss finnishhed. It iss mmy time nnow. MINNNE!"*

"Y-You killed him!" I spluttered.

Grigory's butcher's knife gleamed.

"Hold out your arm," he demanded.

I closed my eyes. I knew I had lost. Death had come for me—

BZZZZZAAAAA!!! BZZZZZAAAAA!!!

Suddenly a piercing wail shook the air. The cabin walls started writhing and shaking. Collapsing.

What was going on? An earthquake? The Apocalypse?

No. My alarm! My genius, once-per-hour alarm!

"Ignore it!" Grigory commanded.

I did the opposite. Blood pulsed in my ears as I focused my will on the noise. The cabin walls dimmed. I was waking up! Leaving this horrible place!

"Nnooooo!" Grigory shrieked. The knife in his hand turned transparent.

Could a transparent knife still draw blood?

I didn't stick around to find out. I leapt backward, just as Grigory lunged with the knife. Wind splashed my arm, shaking the tiny brown hairs that the butcher's knife narrowly missed. Looking back, I saw Grigory's dim face—his sick, one-eyed glare—as both he and the cabin winked out.

I gasped in relief. Home. I was home.

Momentum from the jump sent me staggering forward. My heels skidded on the slick hardwood floor. Against the odds, I'd reached the front door after all—the front door of my house.

I let out a wail as I planted my face on it.

THUMP!

The next thing I knew, Mom was there, dragging me onto my knees.

"Ow." I clutched at my nose. "Ow. Ow. Ow." I felt a trickle of warmth down my face.

"Tammy, you're raining!" Mom gasped.

I touched my nose and felt blood streaming down in thick spurts. I gasped in terror and pain.

A nosebleed.

Mom reached for a napkin. She clamped it over my nostrils, then carefully guided my hand to it.

"Does it hurt, sweetie? Should I call someone? Dr. Lubin? An ambulance?"

"No, please. I'm all right." I crawled to my feet.

"If you say so." Mom sighed. "Hold the napkin tight to your nose, sweetie. Otherwise the bleeding won't stop. What were you doing up this late, anyway?" There was a pause. "Tammy? Are you listening?"

No, I thought. All the sudden, my brain was on fire.

Otherwise the bleeding won't stop.

The bleeding. The blood pouring out of my nose. Human blood.

My heart quivered. Was I crazy? Was I completely insane?

Still squeezing the napkin, I crossed to the kitchen and stretched my arm toward the half-open drawer, ignoring Mom's gasp.

"Tammy, whoa—what are you doing?"

"Just fetching a cup, Mom. I'm thirsty."

"That's a teaspoon, sweetie, not a cup."

"Oh. Haha." My smile stretched crazily, loopily, as I turned toward the stairs. "Thanks for helping me, Mom. You can go back to sleep now. I'll be fine."

Upstairs, I locked myself into the bathroom. I leaned across the sink, shoving the teaspoon up my nose and letting go of the napkin. I started pinching my nostril. Hard. A stinging pain made me gasp. I didn't stop. I kept pinching until the nosebleed restarted, and a syrupy goop filled the teaspoon.

My own blood. Human blood.

One teaspoon down, I thought. *One to go.*

Feeling crazy, completely insane, I dumped the blood in a jar and pinched my nose again.

I DON'T KNOW HOW LONG I stayed awake that night. Minutes? Hours? A full day?

Time seemed to wrinkle and stretch as I lay in bed, trying not to scream for every rattle and thump rising up from the staircase.

Grigory. He was still there. Still chasing me.

"He can't get me," I whispered. "He can't get me here, in my room."

Was it true?

I never found out. A few seconds after speaking, I rolled sideways, squeezing all my blankets and bedsheets around me.

As soon as my face hit the pillow, I died.

37

OKAY, FINE, I DIDN'T die. I fell asleep accidentally—which meant *risking my life*, because the Dream Kitchen could reappear any second.

And Grigory. His freezing, mummy-wrapped hands! His thick knife!

So excuse me, random person, for thinking I died when I sat up in bed and saw a big, popping eyeball, staring at a spot just a foot from my face.

I opened my mouth, ready to scream out in terror. Then the eyeball dipped slightly. A second eyeball appeared. Crisp and light-blue.

Jake Aberforth!

"W-What's going on?" I stammered. "Where am I?"

I looked around and saw an eerie blank space where my bedroom door should be. Jake strolled through the gap, as if nothing was strange.

"D-Did the spell break?" I said. "Is this still my house? Am I…dead?"

A broad grin appeared on Jake's face as he slowly approached me.

No. My nightstand.

He reached for the blood jar I'd left by the clock.

"She did it," he whispered. *"She actually did it…"*

Grinning widely, he snatched it.

What followed was the craziest, loveliest, most impossible night I could ever imagine. What even happened? I remember it only in flashes.

Showing my TammyBakes channel to Jake. Giggling insanely, for almost no reason, before stepping into that eerie blank space.

Where did *that* lead to?

All I really remember is Jake. His sharp grin. The icy chill of his palm gripped in mine. The crisp forest reek as we walked, endlessly walked, until we reached a log cabin as bright as the moon.

"This is my home," Jake announced. "How it was. How it will be again."

Still grinning, he led me inside. Clarisse's Kitchen, said a crisp metal sign on the door. The sweet smell of food pricked my nostrils.

"This way, Tam. Almost there."

We walked past a row of shining glass shelves without cobwebs; down an aisle of sweets, each in fancy domed platters; toward a strange-looking gap in the wall—

A staircase.

I remember thinking to myself, *Haven't I seen this staircase before?*

Jake paused in front of it, grinning like a stop light.

"Just a few more steps, Tam."

Steam from below slammed my nostrils. A warm fragrance flooded into my bones, like a web—like a wonderful web.

I didn't hesitate. I followed Jake down the creaky wood steps.

WE SPENT AGES down there. A full night in the depths of Jake's cabin—a crisp, cozy space that he called "Mother's Kitchen."

Jake was an excellent chef. Whistling merrily, he taught me the steps to an old family recipe. Some kind of cake. Velvet cake? He let me stir the batter and hand-mix the goopy red filling.

The smile never left Jake's face. Not for one second.

Later, his shining eyes lit the street as he walked me home through the darkness.

"I had fun," I said honestly.

"Me too," Jake replied. "Thank you, Tammy. Thank you *so much.*"

Silence fell as we turned up the driveway. The crickets stopped chirping. The frogs held their tongues. The only sound, I think, was the thump of my heart as I realized the only other thing in the dream, the only creature alive, besides me, was Jake Aberforth.

And he was tilting his head. Leaning into me.

Oh God.

My heart panicked. Should I tilt my head? Should I scrunch my lips up? Or not? I didn't know! I'd never done this before. I'd never, well—

THUMP! THUMP! THUMP!

The dream broke like glass, and I woke with a jolt.

What the—?

I rolled around in my sheets, cursing my bad luck. Why did the dream have to end? If only I'd slept for one minute extra. *Or ten.*

"Kiddo?" Dad tapped my bedroom door again. "Your, um, ride is here. Waiting outside. It's, er, kind of a traffic jam, actually."

I rubbed my eyes as honks echoed over the street.

"I think you'd better come down," Dad said wearily.

"Only if she's feeling up to it!" Mom chimed in.

"Even then," Dad muttered, as a pair of voices roared.

"Out of the road!"

"Move it, Jeep! You're blocking America!"

"Okay, okay. Ugh." I rolled out of bed with a groan.

"SURPRISE!" Sheena and Maeve said together. They rushed out of the Jeep like two speeding bullets, hugging me in front of the porch.

"Um, hey guys." I wiggled out of the hug. "What's up? I usually just take the bus."

"Forget the bus," Maeve snorted.

"This is too important," Sheena added. Her silver bracelets clinked as she dragged me into the Jeep. "Like it, Tammy? The Hummer got old, so I made Daddy replace it."

My jaw dropped when I entered the Jeep. The rear cabin was even more stretched than the Hummer. It clogged the driveway and *all* of the street.

"Where's Denise?" I asked, peering round.

"Sick," Sheena and Maeve replied. "Stomach flu." They pulled their phones out and prodded me. "We did what you asked, Tammy. See? We spread your message on text and social media!"

Huh? What were they talking about?

I frowned at Maeve's cell phone screen.

omg yes. literally drooling rn [#TruthOrCake][#CakeFam]
— janet_rox0r
xoxo so excited! beep boop. [#TammyBakesOff]
— a1b2c3_pio
:))) \(=o=)/ [#TammyJakes][#TJForever][#IBelieve]
— emoji_bot_lover

I scrolled, scrolled and scrolled down the comments page until I found the original message that Maeve and Sheena reacted to. It was posted by *ME*, on my TammyBakes channel.

Hello world. Today I write to inform you that I, Tam-myBakes, shall enter the Halloween Bake Off in downtown Hoberville on Saturday, the 31st of October, at one-thirty p.m. In addition, a special preview dessert (a fabulous cake) shall be presented this morning to students and faculty. First come, first serve. Do not miss out.

Warmest regards,

TammyBakes

My eyes bulged. "I-I didn't send that!" I spluttered. "I didn't! I don't even write that way!"

"Don't be embarrassed," Maeve laughed. "It's retro."

"People are super excited," Sheena added.

"B-But I didn't bring them anything! I don't have a *fabulous—*"

HNNNNKK! HNNNKK!

I glanced out the window. Unlike the coupes and sedans, which had either given up or changed course, the school bus was too big to turn around. The bus driver screeched to a halt just a few feet away. She honked again.

HNNNNKK! HNNNKK!

"Um, we'd better go," I said quickly.

"Got it." Sheena slapped her hand on the driver's seat. "Hey! Tammy says step on it!"

A second later, the Jeep roared to life.

THE MIDDLE SCHOOL SIDEWALKS were *packed*. I couldn't believe it. Nearly half of the school had turned out, everyone frantically cheering and waving. There were gasps as we parked and climbed out of the Jeep.

"There she is! My best student!"

"Congratulations, Miss Saris!"

"Your cake—it is simply to die for!"

A knot of faculty pushed to the front, led by Vice Principal McKissock. The teachers held forks and oozing red plates. Behind them stood a fancy domed pedestal, its mat full of crumbs. Only a single red slice lay uneaten.

My heart trembled. *A pedestal…A cake on a fancy domed pedestal…*

I thought back to my dream from last night. To Jake Aberforth and that wonderful, sweet-smelling—

"Oh my God," I said. *"Oh my God!"*

Velvet Cake? Was it Velvet Cake?

No. It was Blood Cake.

38

BLOOD CAKE.

A cake with my blood inside. Human blood.

"Noooo! Get away from the cake! It's not safe!"

I rushed forward, throwing my arms across the Blood Cake's domed pedestal. I had to protect it! This wasn't food you could eat. It was magic. Dark magic!

But what was left to protect?

A single red slice. Thick syrup oozed down the sides. The cake itself seemed to bleed from its knife wounds, as a pale bandage flapped off the glass.

"Is there anything you need, Tammy?" said the voices behind me.

"We're here to help."

"We're your number one fans!"

I rubbed my eyes. My teachers looked so earnest. So helpful. Red ooze stained their lips as they grinned at me.

Servants. They're all servants.

My heart skipped a beat. If my teachers were servants, couldn't I ask them for anything? Unlimited recess. Perfect exam scores. Whatever I wanted, I'd get it.

Any other day, I would've celebrated. Not today. I was scared. The Blood Cake was too gross and too powerful.

Who knew what was going on in my teachers' heads? *Or inside of their stomachs?* They'd just eaten blood! Human blood!

My bones shivered. I knew I couldn't let anyone else eat the Blood Cake. I never even meant to create it. So how did it get here? What happened?

The dream, I thought crazily. *What if Jake and I really did bake a Blood Cake? What if Jake sent the cake to my school? What if Jake took control of my laptop and sent all those messages?*

Jake was in my room, after all. He could have easily done it.

"No, Tammy, he couldn't have," said a voice in my head. "Do you hear yourself right now? Jake isn't a real person. He's a spirit. A ghost. How could a ghost bake a cake and deliver it?"

THE REST OF SCHOOL was a blur. Instead of classes, we held "TammyBakes" sessions, all about me. Kids rearranged their seats so they could sit and gawk at me. Even kids who hadn't eaten my food seemed bewitched, same as everyone else.

This celebrity stuff was contagious.

And, like, super annoying.

"Tammy! Will you enter your cake in the Halloween Bake Off?"

"Tammy! Do you know who the Mystery Judge is?"

"Tammy! Hey! Did you really throw the last piece of cake in the trash? Where, exactly? Which trash can?"

"Shut up, shut up, shut up!" I said finally, crazily.

Guess what happened?

They did. The entire classroom fell instantly quiet. Everyone flashed the same robot smile as Pete. I felt like the last living human in Zombieland.

Not fun.

Not the "fame" I signed up for.

The minute school ended, I raced out the door. I didn't stick around for the bus or the Jeep. I just fled.

Back home, I collapsed on the couch. My plan was to sit and relax. To forget my miserable life for a while. No fans. No celebrity. Absolutely no sneaking into the kitchen.

Should I retire from baking?

Whatever happened, I needed a break. That's what I told Mom and Dad around six o'clock, when they both started yanking me up, off the couch.

"Tammy, move it. We're late."

"The car's running, sweetie."

I rose to my feet with a moan. Believe it or not, there are some things in life that even a celebrity chef can't get out of.

Family stuff. Sibling duties.

A half hour later, I found myself at Pete's fall baseball game, cheering on ten-year-old kids from the stands.

"Go, Pirates!" I yelled. "Go, Pete, go!"

A second later, Pete left his spot on third base. He started climbing the ten-foot steel fence. Trying to 'go', I guess. The rival coach dragged Pete down by his cleats while his son tagged him out.

"Look alive!" I said, later, when Pete started moping.

He instantly dropped to the dirt, shaking his arms, legs and butt, like a worm. He looked alive, all right. I cupped my face in a moan.

When the game ended, Pete led the Pirates team into the stands. A wall of ten-year-olds presented me with their bats, balls and gloves as a gift.

"Game ball, Tammy Saris!"

"Game bat, Tammy Saris!"

"Game sunflower seeds, chewed and spat out, Tammy Saris!"

It was really embarrassing. Especially when the other parents came by, glaring daggers, to ask for their kids' gloves and bats back.

"Keep the seeds," they said. "We insist."

While all of that happened, Mom and Dad spoke to the umpires. One of them turned out to be my math teacher, Mr. Trevors.

My fan.

You can probably guess how *that* went. Mom started gushing as soon as I entered the car.

"Mr. Trevors is really impressed with you, Tammy. Like, *really*. Really, really."

"Frankly, it was kind of alarming," Dad muttered.

Mom shot him a glare. "He seems really excited for you, sweetie. Something about Saturday? Is there a Halloween Bake Off you've entered?"

"Oh. That." My frown deepened. "It's true that I signed up to enter, but I don't think I'm going to. Not anymore."

I might never bake again, I thought grimly.

Silence stretched as our car left the parking lot.

"Sweetie?" Mom said suddenly. "You quit the Bake Off because of your kitchen ban, didn't you?"

I blinked at her.

"Well, surprise! Today's your sunny day!" Mom's eyes gleamed with excitement. "Mr. Trevors told us all about your growing fame as a chef. When we mentioned your ban, he was horrified. He made us promise to let you enter the Bake Off. And guess what? We agreed!"

My jaw dropped. *"You didn't!"*

"We did. We really did!" Mom beamed at me. "I realize we've been a bit hard on you, sweetie. For the record, I disagree with Dr. Lubin's diagnosis. Food poisoning seems a bit of a stretch. What with that stomach bug floating around, your, um, special cookies weren't necessarily at fault. It was likely the bug making all of us ill."

"Yes, the slug," I mumbled. "The stomach slug."

Mom and Dad traded looks. They just laughed.

When we got back, Pete raced upstairs to play Xbox. I moved to follow, but Mom pulled me back.

"It's still early, Tam. You can bake something now, if you like. If you're still feeling up to it."

"Now?" I stared at her. "No way, Mom! Are you crazy?"

She gave me a puzzled look.

"Um, sorry, but I can't. Not tonight. I'm…too tired."

I also need to stay far, far away from the kitchen until I figure out my next move.

I felt a chill down my neck. What could I possibly do? I didn't even know who to trust!

I was halfway up the stairs when Mom's voice drifted up, like a ghost.

"Sweet dreams, Tammy. If you ever need help in the kitchen, I'm here for you, hon. Whatever you need. We could even bake your contest entry together—"

THUMP!

I slammed my bedroom door on Mom's voice. Then I flopped into bed, digging my face in a pillow. I was sick of everything. Sick of celebrity. Sick of baking. Sick of hearing Mom's—

Wait.

I felt a sudden jolt. My door was closed, and the pillow plugged both of my ears. So why did I still hear a voice?

"Together," it said teasingly. "Now that sounds like a nice idea, doesn't it, Tammy?"

My heart stiffened. Slowly, warily, I rolled onto my back. Pushed the pillow away. And found a pair of crisp, light-blue eyes peering down at me.

Jake. He was here.

In my room.

39

I STARED IN HORROR and shock—and okay, maybe the teensiest pinch of delight.

Jake was back. He'd come back!

So why did he look so intense? So alarming?

"H-Howww?" was all I managed to ask him.

Jake grinned at me. A savage light shone in his eyes.

"My spirit is stronger now," he replied. "I can leave *The Booke* much more easily. And it's all thanks to you, Tammy. Thanks to *us.*"

I felt a horrible jolt. *The Blood Cake!*

"*You* wrote the text message," I said slowly. "*You* brought the Blood Cake to school. You told me it was regular cake…an old family recipe…"

"Oh, but it *is.*" Jake's wolf-like grin sharpened. "The Blood Cake and my family go way back. Twenty years? Twenty-five? But enough about me. Are you enjoying your fame, Tammy? How does it feel to be a star on the rise? A celebrity?"

"You…you lied to me! Why did you lie?"

"To save you, Tammy. You were in a dark place. You almost broke your vow to *The Booke of Loste Foodes!* Naturally, I swooped in to help you. To provide a boost of…inspiration."

Jake's light-blue eyes gleamed.

"Didn't we have fun last night, Tammy? I know *I* did. The fun doesn't need to stop there. Take my hand. We can head to the kitchen right now. I know a *wonderful* recipe."

"N-No!" I blurted out. "Please. I don't want to."

Jake clucked his tongue. "Such a pity. Though I can't say I'm surprised." He flicked a finger. "*UP*, Tammy. It's time to get up."

My legs moved abruptly. Within seconds, I was standing up. Walking over to Jake.

I cried out in horror.

"Yes, you're under my Servant Spell," Jake chuckled. "Don't fight it. Escaping the spell is impossible."

"W-W-Why? Why are you d-doing this?"

"I knew you wouldn't join Mother. Not after you struggled with Blood Cake. So we had to improvise. I must say, Tammy, I've always been good at fooling people. I think it's my eyes."

Fooling people…

"Y-You and Chef Clarisse," I said weakly. "You're working together…you were always working together…"

Jake was grinning so widely, I thought his jaw could fall off. I *hoped* it would.

"How much do you know about *The Booke of Loste Foodes?*" he said quietly.

"It's evil," I blurted out. "An evil book full of…evil!"

"Close." Jake licked his lips. "It's a book of witchcraft, Tammy. For witches."

I let out a moan without meaning to.

"I was worried the slugs would tip you off," Jake went on. "If not slugs, then the spiders surely. The blood. The lovely green wart on your forehead." He cackled. "But you exceeded my expectations, Tammy. You truly believed the Grand Desserts were gourmet recipes. You never guessed they were spells. Or that you were slowly transforming. Slowly blossoming…into a witch!"

A witch! A WITCH!

My thoughts spiraled out of control. I started frantically squeezing my forehead wart. Trying to rip it away, like a weed.

Witch. Witch. Witch.

"Nooooooo," I moaned. "You're lying…You're wrong…"

"It's almost over," Jake whispered. "One page left. One dessert until I'm finally healed. I will finally get to join Mother!"

"W-W-What?"

"Twenty years ago," Jake explained, "Mother and I attempted The Final Dessert. We knew the costs going in. We thought we were willing to pay them. On the cusp of success, however, someone's hand slipped—I won't say it was mine—and the recipe backfired. Horribly. As a result, my spirit was violently expelled from my body."

I let out a gasp.

"It's true, Tammy. What you see is only half of me. My better half, actually. I'm afraid my body is a bit…soulless. You wouldn't like him. Although you've met once or twice, I suppose."

Oh my God.

"G-G-Grigory!? Grigory is your body?"

"Grigory is *nothing*," Jake sneered. "He is an empty vessel. Mother's plaything. Even his name is a joke." Jake opened his throat and made a horrible rasping noise (*"Grrriiii…. Griiiii…"*) before he burst into giggles. "His throat is decayed, you see. He struggles with words. Without the mummy wrap, I suppose he would die. Yes. Poor, poor Grigory." Jake's smile widened. "When I am restored, Grigory will cease to exist. It will simply be me. Youthful me. Two-eyed me. Reunited with Mother again. And my lovely, sharp, seven-inch butcher's knife."

Jake flicked a finger. *The Booke of Loste Foodes* appeared in his hand.

"Soon," he said, tapping it. "Soon. Two to go."

"Two?" My heart jolted. "I finished three Grand Desserts. There's one left. You just said that!"

"Of course," Jake replied. "I misspoke."

He walked to the window. The evening wind howled as he pulled my curtains apart.

My jaw dropped. The window was already open. *Again.*

Jake looked delighted. "Good. Very good! I was worried about opening another…passage. Instead, let's make use of this wonderful ladder!"

"Ladder?"

He nodded. "The latch on your window is broken, Tammy. Did you know? Someone has been chipping away at it. My, my. Your stalker is truly efficient!"

My stalker? I thought. *The boy who crashed off the ladder?*

Jake swept his leg across the window ledge. "Oh dear. I almost forgot!" He flung *The Booke of Loste Foodes* at my head. I felt a rush of unknown force as my arms rose to catch it.

"Hold onto that, Tammy. *Keep it secret, keep it safe*—as you follow me out of the house!"

Jake's cold laughter merged with the wind as he climbed out the window. A second later, I followed him out. I had no choice anymore. No control.

I shuddered as my hands and feet touched the ladder.

Where was I going? Where was Jake taking me?

As soon as I asked the question, I knew.

The final ingredient.

My heart trembled. What awful thing were we heading outside, in pitch darkness, to find and collect?

SQUISH. SQUISH. SQUISH.

The wet lawn seeped through my gym socks. We reached the driveway, and black asphalt scraped at my heel.

Shoes. I didn't have them.

"Ow," I moaned. "Ow, ow, ow."

"Less talking, more walking," Jake snapped.

I felt my lips stick together. A ghostly wind howled in my ears as I followed Jake up the sidewalk and out of the neighborhood. One by one, the streetlights fell dark as Jake passed them.

"Faster, Tammy. You won't want to miss this!"

Jake's voice sounded gleeful. I tried to peer through the darkness in front of him. Where were we heading? Why was Jake so excited?

My legs wobbled out of control. Speeding up.

Noooo, I thought. *Don't follow Jake. Don't run after him!*

Teeth clenched, I summoned all my strength, sending it into my legs. I tried to pinch my feet together. To swerve out of Jake's path. To trip and fall, even. So what if my leg snapped in half? At least I couldn't be forced to keep walking.

I was so anxious. So frightened.

There is nothing scarier than being someone else's puppet. It was scary enough when I thought I was dreaming. But now, knowing I was out in the real world, at night...

My heart trembled. *I have to break free,* I thought. *I have to escape the Servant Spell before it's too late.*

I knew it was possible. Hadn't Pete cracked my Servant Spell once?

Yes. But the spell Pete escaped was days old. It had already weakened.

Not mine, I thought queasily. *My spell was created last night, when Jake and I finished the Blood Cake. It's still fresh. At the height of its power.*

How could anyone break it?

"Almost there, Tammy. Can you feel it?"

Jake slid to a halt in a shadowy spot, near some trees. My wet socks touched asphalt, then grass, as I jogged to catch up.

"Where are we?" I mumbled. "I can't see a thing."

"Past the school," whispered Jake. "Past the soccer fields. You remember the forest trail, don't you, Tammy?"

No, I thought. *Please. No.*

"Before we enter, take this."

Jake pressed a broken branch into my palm. I felt its needle-sharp tip and recoiled.

"What the—?"

"Grip it tight," Jake commanded. "Now think back to the page four of *The Booke*. Can you see it now? Do you remember?"

Yes. The vision resurfaced. I could not keep it down.

'I' SCREAM SUNDAY
THE FOURTH GRAND DESSERT

"Excellent." Jake smiled. "Now then. We've come to these woods to find your final ingredient. To hunt and collect it. That's what the stick is for. That's what you'll use."

My whole body shivered. *The final ingredient...*

How could I ever forget it?

FINAL INGREDIENT ALERT!
EYEBALLS (MAMMALIAN, 13CT.)

Of course I'd read the whole recipe. Did you think I left the house without sneaking a look? It was the first thing I did after descending the ladder.

I spent the rest of the walk regretting it.

Eyeballs. Whole eyeballs.

Rotted leaves crunched beneath my socks as I entered the forest. My heart thumped like a drum. I wanted to scream out in panic. To drop the branch Jake had given me. To break the spell and run home.

I didn't want to hunt eyeballs. I didn't want anything to do with the Fourth Grand Dessert. I knew, now, that *The Booke of Loste Foodes* was evil. Pure evil.

Jake laughed out loud when I said that.

"You're so funny, Tammy. You always lighten the mood with your jokes."

I tried to scowl at him. But with the Servant Spell active, I couldn't even do that.

"Why not ask Grigory to help us?" I said randomly. "He seems like the type."

Jake snorted. "Grigory is only good for mindless tasks. Harvesting eyeballs is not mindless. It requires great skill. Living beings are tricky to catch."

Living beings, I thought. My heart jolted.

"You're talking about squirrels! One-eyed squirrels!"

Jake chuckled. "Those squirrels are from a previous harvest. But yes. Squirrels. Rabbits. Deer. Any mammal will do. *Even humans,*" he added, "if any should have the misfortune of stumbling across us tonight, in the dark."

My brain sputtered. *Humans are mammals,* I realized.

Could you really take an eye from a human? A real living person?

NO. No, of course not.

The idea was too sick. Collecting blood was my absolute limit. Everyone gives blood to the doctor sometimes. But *no one* gives eyeballs. Not on purpose. Not willingly.

How would you even…extract them?

My blood chilled as I remembered the branch I was holding.

"The trick," Jake explained, "is to extract a single eye from each victim. A one-eyed creature can still survive in the wild. Trust me. I know."

Trust me. I know. The words lit in my brain, like a torch.

"You sacrificed your own eye!" I blurted out. "Grigory's eye!"

"Yes." Jake smiled coldly. "I did what was required, Tammy. I followed Mother's command. And so what? My spirit body has two eyes. And so shall my true body, once *The Booke of Loste Foodes* is complete, and I successfully…merge. Mother will be so proud of me, then. So delighted!"

Jake's voice trailed away in the wind. Leaving me nauseous.

This family is all kinds of sick, I thought queasily.

Just then, a patch of leaves started shaking. Jake slid to a stop. His light-blue eyes narrowed suspiciously as an unknown voice boomed through the trees.

"You will never escape! You will die a slow, painful death in these woods!"

I suddenly heard a noise like a car engine.

VrrrrRR! VrrrrrRRRRR!

My face paled. *A chainsaw? Was it really a—?*

No. Not a chainsaw.

Of course not.

My heart shivered as I remembered my first walk in these woods, and the scary sound clip that a certain person—an extremely foul, vicious person—had tried to prank me with.

Denise was here? *Denise Daddario?*

My breath quickened.

No. No-no-no. She can't be here. She can't be.

My eyes flicked to Jake. He was squinting into the trees. Slowly tilting his head.

Did he know? Did he realize the voice was a fake?

VrrrrRRRRRR! VrrrrrRRRRRRRRR!

The chainsaw clip played again. Louder now. Closer.

As the leaves rustled, I saw a cherry-red flash.

My eyes popped. Denise's cell phone! She'd left it exposed!

The tiny service light blinked—and Jake pounced.

"Got you!"

"Aaaaahhhhhh!"

Denise gave a shrill scream as Jake seized the scruff of her coat, dragging her out of hiding. She sprawled in the dirt. Moonlight stabbed through the treetops and onto her shivering, horrified face.

"Well, well, well. What a pleasant surprise!" Jake cackled and rubbed his palms together. "This way, Tammy. Come and see what I've caught!"

My legs followed orders. Within seconds, I'd slotted in next to Jake. A savage glee filled his eyes as he turned to me, tapping the branch in my hand. He jerked his thumb at Denise.

At her horrorstruck face.

No. Her eye.

"I'D WONDERED WHEN Tammy's stalker would make an appearance!" Jake said gleefully.

Denise's face was a horrified mask. "You…you're really him…you're not dead…"

She was crawling around, desperate to wriggle away. But how could she?

Jake hauled her onto her knees. He tied her sleeves in a fluffy fur knot before letting her drop again.

"Nooo…Nooo…" Denise kept kicking and thrashing. She wouldn't give up.

"My, my, you *are* persistent!" Jake cackled. "What a shame. You would have made an excellent witch. Although I suppose you still can contribute. In a way. In an eye-popping way. Tammy, *come.*"

I felt my fist lifting into the air. Raising the broken branch toward Denise.

"One," Jake reminded me. "You must only take one."

"One?" Denise squealed. "One of what?"

My face trembled. Fear chewed through my body and into my bones. You can probably imagine how panicked I felt. How afraid. Jake was controlling my limbs! Making me do things!

But what you can't imagine—what shocked even me—was my *other* emotion.

Anger.

Anger and hate.

I stared deeply at Denise's shocked face. She looked so helpless. So pathetic and weak. In my mind's eye, however, I could still see her smug smile. Her twinkling green eyes as she lied to me. Tortured me. Ruined my life.

And for what? A prank? A bit of stupid celebrity?

All the sudden, my blood started boiling.

"T-T-Tammy, what are you doing?" Denise stammered.

"What are YOU doing, Denise?" I snarled back. "Why are you here? Why are you stalking me?"

"B-Because you…you put a spell on me, freak!" An eerie gleam crept into her eyes. "You stole my friends! I scooped slugs in the muck because of you! I even almost swallowed a *witch donut!* Thank God I spit it out. Otherwise I'd be your…your *servant* now, wouldn't I? Oh my God."

Denise laughed hysterically. Manically.

"I knew you never ate that donut," I grumbled.

Denise laughed even harder. "Once I broke your spell," she bragged, "I had to lay low. I couldn't let you boss me around again. So I pretended to be sick with stomach flu. I wasn't, though. I was *investigating*."

She took a quick breath.

"I had to find out how you did it. How you suddenly got so much power. I just never thought the answer would be so…freakish. So you're a witch, Taffy? A real witch?"

I hesitated. *Was I?*

"Nice wart, by the way," Denise sneered. "Can you look somewhere else, please? You're grossing me out."

My eyes burned. I felt fire behind them.

"Oh, are you going to cry now? Get over yourself, Taffy. You're such a freak. I see your stupid, fat eyes. I know how scared you are. Guess what? You should be! I'm going to get myself out of this. When I do, I'm going to punish you. Do you understand? No one messes with Denise Daddario. NO ONE!"

Her shaky voice boomed through the forest. Even her black hair quivered with rage as she crazily balled up her fists.

Jake burst out laughing. "See, Tammy? Now *that* is how a true witch should act! You could learn a thing or two from this girl."

"N-No," I said, shaking. "I'm not like her. I'm *not.*"

"Not yet," Jake said savagely.

My fist moved without warning. The broken branch slashed the air, barely skimming Denise's shocked face.

"Pick a side, Tammy," Jake urged. "Left or right."

My breath quickened. *Left or right? Left or right!?*

I stared at Denise. Her pupils had shrunk to black dots. Purple veins throbbed behind her fragile green irises, as a wet ball of tears drizzled down.

Blood pulsed in my ears. I shut my eyes, pushing the broken branch closer. Barely able to breathe.

Left eyeball? No. Right. Take the right one...

My nerves felt electric. This was it. This was happening.

My right arm crept forward. I braced for impact. The soft squish of wood against—

STOP!

I couldn't do it.

Yes, I hated Denise Daddario. Yes, I wished her all sorts of horrible luck. I'd even put her through horrors already. But no, NO, I did not want her injured. I did not want her losing an eye.

I wasn't a monster.

Not like Jake and his mom.

Don't get me wrong. I wasn't a perfect angel, either. I'd made mistakes recently. Huge ones. My mistakes hurt a lot of good people. And if I'm brutally honest, yes, a part of me *still* wanted the power contained in *The Booke of Loste Foodes*, even now.

I wanted to become a celebrity chef. A world-famous person. An almost Godlike existence, constantly worshiped and watched on TV.

But not like this, I realized.

Not by hurting innocent people. Bewitching them. Transforming them into horrible, zombie-like servants while I sat cozily on my throne made of eyes.

Big, bouncing eyeballs. Green eyeballs.

Sorry. *Lies.* I meant 'lies'.

(I think you still get the concept).

In that moment, a strange sort of clarity jolted my brain. The part of me still obsessed with *The Booke* lost its cold, vice-like grip.

"I don't *need* it," I whispered. "I don't need instant success. I don't need crazy revenge on Denise Daddario. I don't need *The Booke of Loste Foodes* or its mystical power. I can just...let it go."

This is kind of dopey, I know. But as soon as I said it, I felt something shatter inside me.

CRACK!

The Servant Spell broke. Jake let out a moan. He swayed on his feet, looking shell-shocked.

"Y-You...you actually broke..."

My eyes bulged. I was just as astonished as Jake was. Recovering fast, I unclenched my fist and let the broken branch drop. Then I did something truly insane.

I reared back, pulled *The Booke of Loste Foodes* from my pocket, and sent it whizzing into the air, like an oily black missile.

Jake gaped at me. *"I-I-Impossible!"* he cried. *"Y-You're my servant! My dog on a leash!"*

"Sorry, Jake," I replied. "But *I'M* not the one on a leash."

I hope, I thought privately.

And okay, I know what you're thinking.

TAMMY, YOU LUNATIC! WHY DID YOU DO THAT?

I'll try to explain.

For starters, I knew Jake's spirit was tied to *The Booke of Loste Foodes.* Jake could project himself out of its pages, but for how long? How far from *The Booke* could he actually go?

This is where it gets tricky.

Every time I'd seen Jake, he was close to *The Booke*. I'd seen him first at the cabin, when I was physically holding *The Booke*. Later, he'd reappeared at my house—but always upstairs. Always close to my room, where *The Booke* was.

But there were still questions. How had *The Booke* walked itself back to my porch when the pizza guy came, unless Jake put it there? Who brought the Blood Cake into my middle school parking lot, if not Jake? Didn't that suggest Jake could move pretty freely?

No. Not necessarily.

Not if Grigory helped him.

Grigory was Jake's physical body. I didn't truly understand their connection. But I *did* remember a bandage being stuck to the Blood Cake. And hadn't the pizza guy wiped a bandage off *The Booke* when he grabbed it?

If Grigory made those deliveries, not Jake, then maybe Jake's 'leash' to *The Booke of Loste Foodes* was a lot shorter than he'd let me believe.

What really tipped me off, though, was tonight, when Jake made me carry *The Booke* down the ladder and into the forest.

Because why would he do that? Why risk it?

Unless his spirit was still bound to its pages.

Tightly bound. Like a dog on a leash.

But was my theory correct? What if I'd miscalculated?

There was no time to verify anything.

I don't know. Sometimes in life, you just have to put yourself out there. To risk everything on a hunch and a hope. On your own strength—not on anyone else's.

I learned that recently.

Time seemed to lengthen and stretch as *The Booke of Loste Foodes* rose toward the treetops. It crunched through dead leaves. It squeezed between towering branches.

Jake let out a roar, lunging forward. His long fingers grasped for my throat.

I ignored him. My eyes were glued to *The Booke*. Watching it fly. Watching it *missile*. I couldn't believe how far it was going.

Not even Pete could throw a baseball that far.

Probably not even Dad.

I felt an icy chill as Jake reached me. His long fingers curled for my—

"Aaaargggh!" Jake cried suddenly.

He jerked backward, as though pulled by invisible strings. A second later, his pale body fizzed through the branches and leaves. Out of sight.

The Booke had dragged him away, like the servant he was.

It was over.

I let out a huge, gasping breath. Then I looked around for Denise.

She was gone. I found her knotted-up coat in the dirt, near a pile of ruined leaves that marked the spot she'd escaped from.

Good for her, I thought. I was glad nothing terrible happened.

As I turned to go, I saw a faint splash of light, somewhere deep in the woods. Jake's voice wobbled out of it.

"T-Taaammmy!" he cried. "I know you're out there! C-Come back!"

I kept walking.

"C'mon, Tammy! I've seen the way you look at me. We could be more than friends! T-There's chemistry between us. Don't think I've forgotten last night, on your porch!"

Eyeballs, I thought. *Real, living eyeballs. In food.*

"Taaammmmmy! Don't forget the wart on your forehead! You realize that wart is just the beginning, right? Soon your skin will turn putrid. Your nose will twist and deform. Unless you come back and apologize right now, I swear, you'll be a hideous half-witch forever!"

I hesitated.

Eyeballs, I reminded myself. *Living eyeballs. Oven-baked eyeballs.*

I shivered once, then kept walking.

"Taaaaammmmmmy! Wait. Please. I'll do anything! I'll be your servant! I'll eat whatever you give me! And—and Mother can help you! There's more to *The Booke* than you realize. More secrets!"

Eyeballs. Eyeballs. Eyeballs.

By now I was starting to smirk. I was enjoying the weakness in Jake's voice. The desperation. All that junk he said before about persistence, the drive to succeed at all costs or whatever…and *now* look at him.

Begging and pleading for *me* to help. ME.

It was really satisfying.

I reached the school parking lot with a grin on my face. How could I not? Yes, I knew *The Booke of Loste Foodes* was still out there.

I really did want to collect it.

To bury it. Boil it. Burn it to ashes.

Later, I decided. *After Halloween. Once Jake's spirit has weakened.*

My only consolation was that *The Booke* was well-hidden. I'd really thrown it a mile. And anyway, I doubted Jake's spirit had all that much strength left. Even now, his voice was creaking and breaking.

"Taaaaamm—mmmmyyyyy," he croaked in the distance.

I left him like that.

It felt good.

42

NINE DAYS LATER...

"Tammy?" said Dad's voice. "Time to get up, kiddo. Ten o'clock."

"On a *Saturday*," Mom added.

I let out a groan, twisting even deeper under my sheets.

"Don' wanna…" I mumbled. "Wan' sleep…sleep for-eve—UNNGHH!"

I gasped as Pete's hands gripped my pillow and pulled. My eyes flew open. Pete was leaning over me, cringing in horror.

"Oh sick. There's another one!"

Another one? Another WHAT?

I rubbed the sleep from my eyes.

And remembered.

"Peter, stop it!" Mom scolded. "You know your sister is sensitive about her warts—ahem, skin imperfections."

"Never touch a wart, Pete," Dad joked. "They're contagious."

Pete's whole body stiffened. He fled the room with a wail, leaving Mom glaring daggers at Dad.

"What?" he said. "It's the same rule with toads. It's not true?"

"Are you comparing *our daughter's face* to a *toad?*"

Dad's smile flickered. "Think I'd better go."

"Good idea."

A second later, I felt Mom's hand on my forehead. She was lifting my hair. Carefully poking and prodding. *Inspecting.*

"Don't listen to your father, sweetie. You look—er, you look lovely."

"Lovely for a witch!" cackled Pete from the hall.

Mom spun around. For a person without a cucumber nose or a face full of warts, she could sure scare a ten-year-old boy. Pete squeaked and ran off. A second later, Mom started hoisting me up.

"Dr. Lubin will sort your face out on Monday," she promised. "Now c'mon. Up! Halloween only comes around once a year—and the Bake Off is rarer than that!"

HOW AWFUL DID I FEEL? Honestly, not as bad as you'd think. Nine days had passed since that night in the woods, and not a peep from Jake, not a peep from Chef Clarisse or the Dream Kitchen. I'd never felt so relaxed or well-rested since, ever.

I missed the full week of school. Mom told the nurse I was sick, but it wasn't the truth. We both knew the real reason. Face warts. My mossy green, cucumber nose.

In the beginning, Sheena and Maeve called me five times a day. Then it was three times. Then once. Until finally—poof—I was dropped from the group chat.

Too bad, I thought.

But I wasn't surprised. I knew the rules of celebrity. Unless you keep active—post new stuff to your channel, send texts—people start to forget you.

Yes, even your "fans."

And okay, you're probably thinking, "Tammy, isn't that a bit…drastic? Did you really have to quit social media? What about your dream of becoming a celebrity chef?"

And at least one of you will want to add, quietly:

"Don't you still have the Servant Spell?"

Good question. The truth was, I didn't know. More than a week had passed since the Blood Cake incident. I'd already closed my TammyBakes channel and announced my retirement.

Yes. I decided to quit cooking and baking. For now. I wasn't going to track down *The Booke of Loste Foodes*, either.

I'd seen enough.

I was done.

In a few short days, Dr. Lubin would fix my face (without magic) and I'd walk out of his office as a brand-new Tammy Saris. Someone nicer, I hoped. Less wildly famous. Less cruel.

I never wanted to hear the name Aberforth ever again.

DOWNSTAIRS AT BREAKFAST, I tried one last time to convince Mom and Dad to let me stay home, and skip the Halloween Fair.

No luck.

"It was your choice not to enter the Bake Off," Mom lectured. "But you still need to stop in. You promised your teacher."

My lip curled. "Who? Me? I never promised anyone!"

"If you're worried about your physical appearance," Mom went on, smiling, "there's a simple solution."

"Huh? What are you—ARRRGHH!"

I let out a cry as my vision went dark. An unknown object had looped itself over my eyes.

What the—?

I couldn't see anything! I started frantically clawing my head. What was on top of me? What happened? All the while, the object sank lower. Past my lips. Past my neck.

"Help," I gasped. "Can't breathe…it's choking me!"

43

A SECOND LATER, the veil lifted. I could see! I rubbed my eyes and saw Mom, Dad and Pete. They were laughing like crazy.

"Aaaah! So spooky!" said Pete.

"Double, bubble, toil and trouble!" Dad teased.

He tossed me the object he'd pulled off my forehead.

A hat. A big, pointy witch hat.

"Happy Halloween, sweetie," said Mom. "It's a witch costume. Get it?" Beaming, she pinned a billowing cloak to my shoulders.

"It's the perfect disguise for your warts—er, the Halloween Fair," Dad added. "Look on the bright side. You won't even need makeup!"

Pete cackled and tugged at my witch cloak.

"Tammy's a witch! A real wicked witch!"

"No, I'm not!" I slashed out an arm, but Pete was too quick. My heart burned with rage as he skipped around, dodging my fists.

A dark idea filled my head.

Couldn't I *make* Pete stand still, if I wanted? Couldn't I use the Servant Spell and force him to freeze? To bang his head on a wall? To drop dead?

My lips parted. The command was on the tip of my tongue.

No! I thought suddenly. *You're not a witch, Tammy. Not anymore.*

Letting Pete slip away, I ripped the cloak off and dumped the hat on the floor. I took big, calming breaths.

"If I have to go the Halloween Fair, then fine," I said. "But I'll wear something else."

THE HALLOWEEN FAIR TOOK place in the Hoberville Middle School parking lot. This year, even Main Street was packed. Bodies spilled past the sidewalks and into the streets. It was really surprising.

"Tammy, Pete, end of the line," Dad announced.

The car doors swung open in the middle of Main Street.

"You're dropping us off?" I said.

"No choice," Dad sighed. "Your mom and I will try to park and come find you. If we're not back in thirty minutes, look for us in the fifty-car pile-up."

"Keep an eye on your brother," Mom warned me. "He's too young to be walking alone."

Pete and I waved as the car lurched away, at the speed of molasses. We were still waving ten seconds later. Finally, we gave up. That's when Pete made a run for it.

"Later, dork. I've got plans."

"Pete! Stop!" I cried out, without even thinking, as he pushed through the crowd in his costume (a dusty, bee-yellow Pirates uniform). My heart chilled as I realized what I'd just done.

A command. I'd given Pete a command.

I held my breath, waiting for Pete to freeze like a statue. Would he trip and fall? Cause a traffic jam?

No. He kept walking.

I let out the breath I didn't even know I was holding.

It's over, I thought. *The Servant Spell is gone. It's all over.*

A moment later, I adjusted my "costume" (an old catcher's mask that Pete used to wear) then joined a long line of kids pushing toward the middle school. Everyone seemed really excited. Loud voices carried over the Halloween music and footsteps.

"I can't believe how big the crowd is!"

"Because of TammyBakes, do you think? Is she here?"

"No, Alan. TammyBakes is old news. Check the poster."

One of the boys nodded to a sign pasted onto a streetlight. My heart skipped a beat as I read it.

MYSTERY JUDGE UNMASKED!
Master Chef J.B. Carcetti
– 10-time Chef Weekly winner
– Host, Restaurant Battle TV Show

LOCATION:
The Halloween Bake Off Tent!
(Field 2C, Hoberville Middle School)

SCHEDULE:
Autographs 10am–1pm
Bake Off Judge 1:30pm–2pm

Underneath was an image of a chubby man with a lizard-green mohawk. He flashed his signature move, a thumb and pinky salute.

"Huh," I mumbled. "So the mystery judge is J.B. Carcetti."

Overhearing, the group of boys whipped around.

"Amazing, right? J.B.C. owns about a hundred restaurants!"

"He's on TV like twenty-four seven."

"Those contestants are lucky. If J.B.C. likes their food, he'll definitely invite them onto his show. The winner could become a star overnight—just like *that!*"

The boy, Alan, snapped his monster-gloved fingers. The noise came out as a dull scrape. Everyone pointed and laughed at him.

Not me.

Frowning, I pushed ahead of them. I felt a twinge of regret in my heart. How many times had I seen that chubby-cheeked, mohawk-haired face on a cookbook front cover?

J.B. Carcetti...

With a celebrity like J.B.C. supporting me, the sky was the limit. I could've gone pretty far, as a chef...

"Oh well," I sighed, pushing on—

THUMP!

And straight into Vice Principal McKissock. She let out a gasp, then turned to stare at me. My whole body stiffened. I cowered behind the bars of Pete's catcher's mask.

"Ann?" said a voice. "Is something wrong?"

I peeked up and saw my science teacher, Mr. Murray. Vice Principal McKissock turned back to him, shaking her head.

"Apologies. I thought I saw—well, doesn't matter. As I was saying, Fred, I just wanted to apologize for the, er, incident in your science lab. The break-in."

"Oh, it's quite all right—" Mr. Murray started to say.

"Rumors are flying, of course," Ms. McKissock cut in. "They're saying that *frogs* were released in the pipes. That they're hopping up out of, well...*toilets*." Her voice dropped to a whisper. "There isn't any truth to that last part, I hope?"

"Never fear, Ann, your bottom is safe—and frog free!" Mr. Murray tapped his beard stubble, chuckling. "Number one, I never kept frogs. They're American Toads. Number two, my toads were dead when I bought them. How can you bring the dead back to life? Now there's a trick I'd pay to see happen!"

"So it's, er, impossible, then? Just a joke?"

Mr. Murray grinned at her. "My students tend to exaggerate. It's one of their better qualities. I'm just surprised they focused on frogs this time. There were other things stolen out of that fridge, you know. Campbell's soup. Snickers bars. A sealed container of cow eyes."

Ms. McKissock gasped. *"Cow eyes?* What do you mean, cow eyes?"

Mr. Murray beamed. "For dissection!"

As Ms. McKissock gasped again, I felt a chill down my neck. The prickly feeling in my heart turned into a full-blown explosion.

The science lab was robbed.

A bunch of cow eyes were missing.

My heart raced as I worked through the implications of that sentence. Cows were mammals, right? Which meant that their eyes...If you had enough of them...If you dumped them into a mixing bowl...

No, I thought. *The Booke of Loste Foodes is gone. Lost and buried. So who could've possibly baked the Fourth Grand Dessert? The 'I' Scream Sunday?*

I felt a horrible jolt.

Was it me? Did I do it?

"No," I mumbled. "Of course not. Ridiculous!"

Right?

I stood there, shaking like a leaf. I'd never felt so queasy in my life. Did I really return to those woods? Did I steal back *The Booke?* Rob the science lab?

In a dream, did I sneak my way back to that...kitchen?

NO. I refused to believe it! I was sure I would've remembered the dream, if I did that.

"Not all dreams get remembered," said a voice in my head.

I shivered again. I clutched my chest, trying to calm my beating heart. My lungs spasmed. When had I started gasping?

I choked and looked up.

Where was Vice Principal McKissock rushing off to?

I watched as she pushed through the crowd, toward the Bake Off tent. My math teacher, Mr. Trevors, quickly passed her a note and a megaphone. A second later, her cold voice rang out like a thunderclap:

"CONTESTANT #13—TAMMY SARIS!"

Oh my God.

There were cheers as she added, "This is our final plate of the day, folks. Your winner will be announced after this, so watch closely!"

My throat tightened. I stood stiffer than wood as Ms. McKissock presented a tiny domed plate to the judges panel. I watched it bobble around, passing one to another, until it finally stopped. A large man with a two-foot-tall, lizard-green mohawk jumped up.

"My turn, baby. Rock on!"

Chef Carcetti saluted the crowd, pinky-first.

Then he raised his dessert fork.

"NO!" I GASPED. "Don't eat it! Whatever's on the plate, throw it out!"

Nobody listened. Whispers spread like hissing fires as everyone craned their necks toward the Bake Off Tent.

"Where is she? Where's Tammy?"

"Forget Tammy. Check out Tammy's dessert!"

"One slice? Is it only one slice?"

"Haven't I seen this dessert before?"

My legs shook as I pushed toward the tent. I almost tripped and fell over. But I couldn't stop. I had to see the dessert that I'd somehow entered into the Bake Off.

But how did I bake it?

My brain was spinning out of control. I was so dizzy, I almost steamrolled a family of four. As they squealed and escaped, I pushed through the gap where their stroller had been.

The Bake Off tent rose into view. I squinted my eyes through the catcher's mask.

Red. The serving plate oozed cherry-red.

Blood Cake!

I gasped in relief. "Oh thank God." So it wasn't the 'I' Scream Sunday. I hadn't secretly baked the Fourth Grand Dessert in a dream. Thank the Lord!

So then who brought the Blood Cake slice? Jake?

No. Jake was trapped in the woods.

I racked my brains, thinking back to that morning at school, when the Blood Cake appeared. All my teachers had eaten some. There was barely any left when I'd finally arrived.

Except for one slice.

The slice I'd dumped in the trash.

My heart jolted. *Vice Principal McKissock! She must've pulled the slice out of the trash can. She entered it into the contest!*

Was it possible? Could she really do something so…gross?

Yes, I thought crazily. *If she was one of my fans. Absolutely.*

Up on stage, Chef Carcetti raised a forkful of cake to his mouth. "Don't eat it!" I hissed. But too late. He was already chewing.

In an instant, his stout body stiffened. A wave of energy rushed through his cheeks—up his lizard-green hair—into the bowling ball trapped in his stomach.

I stood frozen in shock—*and excitement.*

Yes, I'd sworn not to use *The Booke of Loste Foodes* in the future. But the Blood Cake was an *old* recipe. I baked it days ago. So if Chef Carcetti liked it—if he put me on his TV show, launching me into superstardom—was it really my fault?

No. Of course not!

I mean, why *shouldn't* I take advantage of the situation? I could un-retire. I could reinstate TammyBakes and be famous again.

Famous and rich.

Best of all, I wouldn't even have to feel guilty about it.

Blood, I reminded myself. *He ate human blood.*

A shiver ran through me. Suddenly I didn't know *what* to think.

Looking up, I saw Chef Carcetti smiling and rubbing his belly. He was making a big show of things. Getting the crowd riled up.

Finally, he delivered his verdict.

"Hoooo, mama. Now *that* is a killer confection. Such flavor. Such texture!" He licked a syrup smear off of his lips. "I give it a solid B+. Really good, but not quite the best."

My eyes almost popped and fell out. *Not the best?*

The judges huddled together.

"Second place," Ms. McKissock announced. "Tammy Saris!"

Her words left me groggy and stumbling around. I never thought the Blood Cake could lose. What could beat Blood Cake?

Restless, I pulled off my catcher's mask. I suddenly couldn't breathe. Couldn't think.

"Ahhh!" someone shrieked.

"Monster! Witch!" cried another.

They pointed up at my face. As the crowd panicked, unsure what to do, a girl in glossy gym shorts swooped in, followed by a girl with huge, clinking bracelets. They grabbed hold of my arms, pulling me forward.

"Say cheese, Taffy."

"Ugh, Maeve! That was *my* line!"

My vision blurred as I wobbled along. My brain felt like syrupy goo.

"Eat something, Taffy. You'll feel better."

Before I could gasp, there was food in my mouth. Someone was jamming it in. Eyes popping, I crazily swished it around.

The first thing I felt was the SQUISH! of syrupy ooze.

Then came a POP! like a gumball exploding.

Shrill laughter surrounded me. Someone shoved a serving plate into my hand. I stared at it.

Cold, smushy ice cream. A half-eaten cupcake. And eyeballs. Cow eyeballs.

I felt a fierce wave of horror and shock.

And then, moments later...

"Ohhhhhh!" I moaned with delight.

The taste! The extraordinary taste!

I downed the rest of the plate in one slurp, like a vacuum cleaner, then slowly opened my eyes.

Someone was standing next to me. Her green eyes twinkled, like emeralds, as her perfect lips curved in a smile that ran to her ears.

An angel, I thought. *An angel is shining down on me.*

My breath caught in my throat as she laughed.

"Gotcha, Tammy."

EPILOGUE

TWELVE-YEAR-OLD DENISE DADDARIO could barely believe her green eyes.

"It worked! The Fourth Grand Dessert really worked!"

"Of course it worked," said the voice in her pocket. *"Didn't I swear that it would? Don't you trust me?"*

Denise's grin flickered. "Yes. Of course, Jake. I trust you."

"Good. Now hurry back to the cabin. Bring Tammy."

"Bring Tammy?"

"The Final Ingredient."

"Oh! Right!" Denise tightened her grip on Tammy's wrist. She cringed a little, just touching the girl. All those warts. And that coat hanger nose.

"Geroff me!" Tammy struggled. "Let go!"

"Stop twisting!" Denise spat.

Tammy's body fell instantly limp. She stopped struggling.

"Much better." Denise tossed her perfect black hair with a sneer. "Follow me, *servant*. I don't care if your legs hurt. We're walking."

They reached the edge of the forest in seconds. Denise gave a wild laugh. She'd never felt so strong. So important.

UNTIL RECENTLY, Denise's greatest accomplishment was building her Circle Girls web channel. She was enormously proud of it—even if she'd stolen most of her ideas from other peoples' accounts.

That was just business, after all. It was just being smart.

But she would have to revise her Wikipedia page now. Because nothing could compare to this feeling. This brilliance. This power. Her new greatest accomplishment, without doubt, was going back into the woods to retrieve *The Booke of Loste Foodes*.

The ghost boy, Jake Aberforth, was ever so kind. His light-blue eyes burned like flames as he vowed to help Denise rise to power and fame. To *celebrity*. All it took, he explained, was four simple foods. Four desserts. Denise wouldn't even have to bake them herself, so long as she found some specific ingredients.

And she had.

One by one.

It burned her up that Tammy Saris, that freak, had nearly stolen her spotlight. But Tammy was too weak in the end. She didn't have the guts to complete *The Booke of Loste Foodes*.

Denise did.

Denise was smarter than Tammy. She had more strength. More ambition.

When Denise put her mind to a goal, she accomplished it.

Always. No matter the cost.

"THROUGH HERE," SAID DENISE. "Past the cobwebs. Down the creaky wood steps."

Denise sneered as she watched Tammy waddle along, like a duck on a leash. Should she also tell Tammy to quack? To slap her own face? Eat a cobweb?

Tempting. So tempting.

"Am I...dreaming? Tammy said sleepily.

Denise giggled. "No, Tammy. This isn't a dream. We're just having a little walk down some steps. To a kitchen." Her lip curled. "It's right here. Did you know? The kitchen was always right here. In the cabin."

"I didn't know," Tammy slurred. "Jake never told me."

"Poor Tammy. Jake never trusted you, did he? Not the way he trusts me. I bet he never mentioned the Final Dessert to you, either."

Denise swore she saw chills running down Tammy's neck.

"Th-The Final Dessert?"

"Oh yes. *And* its final ingredient." Denise cackled. She felt a surge of excitement as she descended the creaky wood steps. Tammy doddered behind. Her fat feet slapped the wood like bananas.

When Denise reached the bottom, a thousand smells filled her nostrils.

All of them sweet.

All enticing.

"Here I am," she announced. "Hi, Grigory. Hi, Chef Clarisse. I did as you asked. I brought Tammy."

Denise reached out and shoved Tammy ahead of her, into the light. She enjoyed the slack-jawed look on Tammy's face when she spotted the mummy chef, Grigory. He looked ready to spring at her!

No. At the last moment, Chef Clarisse pulled him back. She swept forward, looking regal and slim in her pearly-white witch robes. Or were they chef's robes? Denise couldn't quite tell the difference.

"At last! At long last!" Beaming, Chef Clarisse snatched *The Booke of Loste Foodes* from Denise. Her thin fingers tickled the binding. For a long time, she didn't speak.

"Please, can we bake now?" Denise interjected. "I want to finish this. I want to be famous. And gorgeous. And rich."

Chef Clarisse wasn't listening. Her red eyes flicked from Grigory to the glossy projection beside him. Jake Aberforth's spirit. His ghost.

"Are you ready, my son? This is our last step. The dessert we failed to condense twenty years ago. There was a hiccup, then. Do you remember it?"

"Yes, Mother," said Jake.

"Yssss," Grigory rasped. *"Reunite usss. It'sss time."*

Chef Clarisse flicked a finger. A glossy black page hovered into the air. "Twenty years ago, this page was accidentally severed from *The Booke*. It, too, must be reunited with its physical form. Reinserted into *The Booke*. To do so requires a…*sacrifice*."

Denise coughed and stepped forward. She didn't like being kept out of conversations. This was a special time for her, too. The culmination of all of her work. So why should Chef Clarisse get to hog it?

"I did my part," Denise reminded them. "I brought you your final ingredient."

Denise suppressed a chill as she pushed Tammy toward Chef Clarisse. She tried not to think about what she was doing. She kept her focus ahead. On celebrity life. On the future.

Although Jake had trusted Denise, he hadn't shown her the full Final Dessert. All he'd let her see was one section. Two narrow lines in a box.

FINAL INGREDIENT ALERT!
WITCH (FULLY BLOSSOMED, 1CT.)

Denise's throat clenched as Chef Clarisse advanced on her. She tried not to think about Tammy. Deep down, she knew she was making the right choice. The smart choice. Sometimes a sacrifice had to be made. Not everyone could be a winner, like Denise Daddario.

"Thank you, child. You have indeed done your part." Chef Clarisse grinned at Denise. Then she turned to the mummy chef, Grigory. "Take her."

Denise's green eyes twinkled. "Allow me." She opened her mouth, ready to call Tammy forward. But what came out of her throat was a scream.

"Aaaaahhhh!"

She felt the chill of Grigory's hand on her wrist. Jerking her forward.

"N-Not me!" Denise wailed. "T-Take *her!* T-Take the witch!"

Chef Clarisse only laughed.

"Oww!" howled Denise. "Jake! Jake! Make him stop!"

Jake's light-blue eyes crinkled. "Why don't *you* stop, Denise?"

At these words, Denise's whole body stiffened. Her last gasp died in her throat. She could not even scream as Grigory led her deeper into the kitchen, toward a serving bowl shaped like a skull. The insides glittered with cherry-red icing.

Chef Clarisse tittered. "Alas, Tammy Saris is no witch. She failed to blossom. She never completed the Four Grand Desserts. *But you did.*"

"No," said Denise. "Stop. Please."

She lurched to a halt in front of the skull-shaped bowl. Freezing air wafted up, sending chills through her eyes as Grigory shoved her neck lower.

And lower.

Until her every breath filled with icing.

"The Soul Sorbet," Chef Clarisse announced. "A deceptively simple dessert. And yet the true cost is enormous."

Tears filled her eyes as she glanced at Jake first, then to Grigory. There was a story there. Something dark. Something twisted.

Denise would never learn what it was.

"Twenty years I have waited!" Chef Clarisse's voice boomed. "Twenty years to finish *The Booke of Loste Foodes*. To correct my mistake. To bring my only son, Jake, back to life!"

With a loud cackle, she slid the glossy black page toward *The Booke*.

SOUL SORBET
THE FINAL DESSERT

There was a loud CRACK! as *Booke* and page reunited. The frost on Denise's eyelashes thickened. Trembling beneath a mask of icing and snow, she said, "H-How? H-How could this happen?"

"Secrets for another time. Another life!" Beaming, Chef Clarisse snapped her fingers. "Grigory! Jake! It is time."

There was a hideous cackle. The pressure on Denise's neckbone increased as a blast of sweet-smelling air slammed her nostrils, one last time. A horrible coldness ran through her.

Then nothing.

FIVE MINUTES LATER, Chef Clarisse set the finished Soul Sorbet on the counter. The child's horrified face was perfectly preserved. A picture of beauty and terror.

The perfect dessert.

Behind her stood an extraordinarily handsome boy with wavy brown hair and piercing, bright-blue eyes. He was flexing his arms. Feeling the warmth and blood as it rushed through his veins.

There was nothing ghostly about him.

"Hello, Mother," he said lightly.

Chef Clarisse wiped a tear from her eye. Her chef's hat tipped to the floor as she leapt forward. Jake. Her own Jake. They embraced for a very long time. And then…

"*Taaaaammmmy.*"

A soft voice drifted over the kitchen. It wound its way between thick puffs of sweet-smelling fog, toward the panicked and shivering girl at the foot of the staircase.

"*Taaaaammmmy,*" it repeated. "Don't be alarmed, child. Sit. Sit. Aren't you hungry? Why don't you come a bit closer, and have a look at the bowl?"

ALSO BY SCOTT CHARLES

Read the rest of the Creeptown series!

THE FINAL INGREDIENT
THE BONE TAKER
THE BREAKING GAME (SUMMER 2021)
TECH SUPPORT (A CREEPTOWN SHORT STORY)

Or check out my other books! (Okay. One book.)

MYLO AND MAX BREAK THE WORLD

What? You've already read them? No? You're too AFRAID to read more? Look, I get it. No judgment! But in that case, you should *definitely* find me online at www.Scott-Charles.com and add your name to…

THE SCOTT CHARLES NEWSLETTER!

Get the knowledge you need to stay far, far away from future Creeptown releases, as well as other thrilling, no-nonsense books about tough situations, such as Pixie infestation and piano recitals gone wrong, which are, quote, *"just too intense for my William. No thank you!"*

ABOUT THE AUTHOR

SCOTT CHARLES is the author of *Creeptown*, a horror adventure series for young readers, and the standalone adventure *Mylo and Max Break the World*. He writes thrilling books for busy kids who might not want to be reading, but what choice do they have? Zero! None!

Scott grew up in a pair of small towns outside of Princeton, New Jersey. He attended Duke University, where he graduated with a B.A. in Public Policy and successfully summoned [REDACTED]. He enjoys the spoils of his dastardly deal at his home in Charlotte, North Carolina. You can find him at the library, across a chess board, or on a soccer field late, late at night.